Please return / renew this item by last
date shown. Books may also be renewed
by phone or the Internet.

THE
MARRIAGE
BETRAYAL

THE
MARRIAGE
BETRAYAL

BY

LYNNE GRAHAM

First published in Great Britain 2011
by Mills & Boon, an imprint of Harlequin (UK) Limited.
Large Print edition 2011
Harlequin (UK) Limited, Eton House,
18-24 Paradise Road, Richmond, Surrey TW9 1SR

© Lynne Graham 2011

ISBN: 978 0 263 22240 1

Harlequin (UK) policy is to use papers that are natural,
renewable and recyclable products and made from
wood grown in sustainable forests. The logging and
manufacturing process conform to the legal environmental
regulations of the country of origin.

Printed and bound in Great Britain
by CPI Antony Rowe, Chippenham, Wiltshire

PROLOGUE

'I DON'T *do* English country weekends,' Sander Volakis informed his father without hesitation.

With difficulty, Petros Volakis mustered a diplomatic smile, wishing for the hundredth time since the death of his eldest son that he had devoted a little more time and attention to his awkward relationship with his younger one. After all, on the face of it, Lysander, known as Sander to his friends, was a son that any man would be proud to possess.

Extremely good-looking and athletic, Sander had a shrewd brain for business and his outstanding entrepreneurial skills had already ensured that even without family backing he excelled at making money. Unhappily, however, Sander also had a darker side to his passionate temperament and a wild streak that ran deep. He was obstinate as a rock, arrogant and fiercely independent, indeed very much an extrovert individualist in a family of unashamedly conservative people. Over the years clashes between father and son had proved inevitable because Sander went his own way...*always*. Parental disapproval had not deterred him. But with the death of Titos, Sander's older brother, the need to build bridges had increased a thousandfold, Petros reflected heavily.

'Eleni's family deserve to see you visit their English home again as a guest,' Petros argued. 'It's not their fault that your brother died in the car crash and that his fiancée survived—'

Sander elevated a contradictory brow, his lean darkly handsome features grim while a glow of disagreement burned bright in his dark gaze. 'Eleni only just escaped a charge of careless driving—'

'They went out in Eleni's car, so she was at the wheel!' Petros snapped back at his son, frustrated by his unforgiving attitude. 'It was a snowy night and the roads were treacherous. Have a little compassion and make allowances for human error. Eleni was devastated by Titos' death.'

Not so devastated that she had resisted the urge to flirt with his younger brother within weeks of Titos' funeral, Sander recalled with cynical cool. But he kept that salient fact to himself, well aware that his parent would gallantly protest that Sander must have misinterpreted her signals. Although only six months had passed since Titos' demise, Sander had already become bleakly aware that that tragic event had transformed his prospects in the eyes of his peers. As his shipping tycoon father's only surviving heir, he was now viewed as a much bigger catch than when he'd been seen as a mere maverick businessman cut loose from the family apron strings.

'Relations between our respective families will relax again if you accept the invitation to stay at the Ziakis home,' Petros declared.

Sander gritted his even white teeth, resenting the request, for he had no desire to fill his late brother's shoes in any way. He liked his life just as it was and wondered if his parents were cherishing the ludicrous hope that he might miraculously warm to Eleni and marry her because she was an equally good catch in shipping terms. He almost winced at so depressing a prospect. Eleni might be beautiful and accomplished, but at twenty five years of age Sander had not the smallest desire to marry or settle down with one woman and his headline-grabbing private life remained as varied and adventurous as he could make it.

'I would really appreciate this, Sander,' the older man declared in a grudging undertone that hinted at how hard he found it to ask for a favour.

Sander studied the older man, reluctantly noticing the lines of age that grief had indented more heavily on his face. He was disturbed by that pull on his conscience and loyalty. But he could not fill the hole that Titos had left in their family. Having been the indisputable favourite from birth, his older brother would be an impossible act to follow. Sander had always refused to compete with his sibling because when he was quite young he had noticed that it had annoyed their parents when he'd outshone their firstborn.

But what the hell was one weekend if it made his parents content that the social mores they based their entire lives on had been respected? Sander asked himself in sudden exasperation.

'All right, I'll go…this once,' he felt moved to add, afraid that he might be creating a precedent and setting himself up for other boring social occasions.

'Thank you. Your mother will be relieved. You're almost certain to meet friends at Westgrave Manor and no doubt useful business connections as well,' Petros continued, conscious that his son's primary need to forge his own power base and fortune were more likely to influence him than anything else.

In the wake of that uncomfortable meeting neither man was best pleased with the other. Driven now by a desire to do his duty, Sander proceeded to an upper floor in the Athens town house to visit his grieving mother, Eirene. On his way his mobile buzzed and he checked the number: Lina, his current lover; this was already her *third* call since he'd left London. He switched his phone to silent, resolving to ignore her and ditch her at the first chance he got. A sense of injustice dogged him, though. What was it that turned women from exciting lovers into all-too-predictable demanding stalker types in search of a commitment he had already made clear he wasn't offering?

As usual, his mother lamented Titos' death as if it had only just happened. Sander submitted to being wept over and reproached for his deficiencies in comparison to his perfect brother before finally beating the fastest possible retreat back to the airport and the freedom that he revelled in. He knew it would be quite a few months before he could make himself visit again; going home was *always* a downer in his view.

CHAPTER ONE

'OF COURSE you should go and take the opportunity to get to know your sister better,' Binkie pronounced, beaming at the prospect of Tally being treated to a luxury weekend in a stately home. 'You could do with a break after all the studying you've been doing.'

Unsurprised that the older woman had taken only the most positive view of the invitation, Tally swallowed back the admission that her father's phone call and request had come as an unwelcome surprise. She pushed her honey-blonde curls off her brow with a rueful hand, her green eyes wary. 'It's not quite that simple. I got the impression that my father only wants me to go so that I can police Cosima's every move—'

'My goodness,' Binkie cut in with a frown of dismay. 'Did he say so?'

'Not exactly.'

'Well, then, aren't you being a bit too imaginative?' Binkie asked in gentle reproof, her kindly brown gaze resting on the younger woman's troubled face. 'Granted your father rarely gets in touch but why immediately assume the worst of his motives? Maybe he simply wants his two daughters to get to know each other.'

'I'm twenty years old and Cosima's seventeen—if that's what he wants why would he have waited so long?' Tally responded wryly because, after a lifetime of disappointments and hurtful rejections, she was a dyed in the wool cynic when it came to either of her parents.

Binkie sighed. 'Perhaps he has seen the error of his ways. People can mellow as they get older.'

Reluctant to parade her bitterness in front of the woman who was the closest thing she had ever had to a loving mother, Tally stared a hole in the table because Binkie was always an optimist and Tally was reluctant to make yet another negative comment. Binkie or, to be more formal, Mrs Binkiewicz, a Polish widow, had looked after Tally since she'd been a baby and had soon graduated from childcare to taking care of her employer's household as well. Anatole Karydas was a very wealthy and powerful Greek businessman who had done his best to ignore his eldest daughter's existence from birth. He hated Tally's mother, Crystal, with a passion and Tally had paid the price for that hostility. Crystal had been a well-known fashion model, engaged to Anatole at the time that she'd fallen pregnant...

'Of course I planned it!' Crystal had admitted in a rare moment of honesty. 'Your father and I had been engaged for over a year, but his precious family didn't like me and I could see that he was going cold on the idea of marrying me.'

As, in the midst of that delicate situation, Crystal had been caught cheating with another man, Tally could only feel that her father had had some excuse for his waning matrimonial enthusiasm. Indeed, her parents had such different outlooks on life that she did not see how they could ever have made each other happy. Anatole, unfortunately, had never been able to forgive or forget the stinging humiliation of her mother's betrayal or the embarrassing interviews she had sold to magazines maligning him in the aftermath of their break-up. He had also questioned the paternity of the child that Crystal was carrying. Ultimately, Crystal had had to take her ex-fiancé to court to get an allowance with which to raise her daughter and although her father had eventually paid his dues Tally had reached eleven years of age before he finally agreed to meet her. By that stage, Anatole had long since married a Greek woman called Ariadne with whom he'd also had a daughter, Cosima. Tally had always been made to feel that she was on the outside looking in and surplus to paternal requirements.

In fact she could count on two hands the number of times she had met her reluctant father. Currently a student in her last year of a degree course in interior design, however, Tally was conscious that Anatole *had* paid for her education and she was grateful for that because her spendthrift mother never had a penny to spare at the end of the month.

'You like Cosima,' Binkie pointed out cheerfully. 'You were really pleased when you were invited to her seventeenth birthday party last year.'

'That was different. I was a guest,' Tally pointed out ruefully. 'But my father made it clear on the phone that he was asking me to accompany Cosima this weekend to keep her out of trouble. Apparently she's been drinking and partying too much and seeing some man he disapproves of.'

'She's very young. Naturally your father's concerned.'

'But I don't see how I could make a difference. I doubt very much if she would listen to me. She's much more sophisticated than I am and very headstrong.'

'But it's heartening that your father trusts you enough to ask you to help, and Cosima does like you…'

'She won't like me much if I try to interfere with her fun,' Tally retorted wryly, but she was far from impervious to the sound good sense of Binkie's reasoning.

In truth, after a couple of brief encounters, organised mainly to satisfy the younger woman's lively curiosity, Tally was the one still intrigued by her beautiful ornamental half-sister, who regularly appeared in the gossip columns rubbing shoulders with the rich and famous. The two young women had nothing in common in looks or personality and lived in different worlds. Cosima was the much loved and indulged daughter of a very rich man. She wore designer clothes and jewellery and was only seen out at the most fashionable social venues. The tougher realities that had shaped Tally and formed her attitudes had never touched Cosima, who had been cocooned in privilege from the day she was born. Cosima had never had to deal with unpaid bills or bailiffs or a mother who, when the cupboards were bare, would buy a new dress instead of food. Only the roof over their heads remained safe because the terraced town house in London where Tally lived with her mother and Binkie was an investment property belonging to her father.

It was there that the limousine called just over a week later to collect Tally. Having handed the driver a small weekend bag to stow away, she scrambled into the rear seat where her half-sister subjected her to a pained appraisal. 'You're dressed all wrong,' Cosima complained, viewing Tally's colourful raincoat and jeans with a grimace.

'I have a typical student wardrobe and two business suits bought for my work experience last year and that's pretty much it,' Tally told her frankly, studying Cosima who was an extremely pretty girl with long black hair and big brown eyes, her slim figure beautifully set off by a fashionable mini dress and perilously high heels. 'You look like you're about to go out on the town.'

'Of course. Some of the most eligible young men of my generation will be staying at Westgrave this weekend,' Cosima remarked and then her vivacious face split into a huge grin. 'You should see your face! That was me quoting Dad. He'd love to marry me off to some filthy-rich guy so that he could stop worrying about me. But I've already got a man.'

'Great. Who is he?' Tally enquired with interest and the lively enthusiasm that was the mainspring of her personality. She was grateful the attention was off her clothing deficiencies, because that so-visible difference between them had embarrassed her.

'His name's Chaz and he's a DJ.' Cosima veiled her gaze, her reluctance to share any more personal facts palpable. 'Are you seeing anyone?'

'Not right now, no,' Tally fielded, her face warming when she thought about how long it was since she had gone out on a date. But then she loathed it when men she barely knew tried to paw her and was even more turned off when the same men were drunk. Finding a comparatively sober male on a night out, she had learned, was a challenge.

Being raised by a devoutly religious and moral woman like Binkie had put Tally rather out of step with her contemporaries. But having lived through the constant turmoil caused by her mother's colourful love life, Tally had embraced Binkie's outlook with gusto. Although now in her forties, Crystal remained a very beautiful woman. But none of her relationships had lasted, most of them being based on the most superficial male attributes and desires. Standing on the sidelines of such shallow affairs, Tally had long since decided that she wanted something more than just lust, a good laugh or an open wallet from a man, and she told herself that she was quite happy to sleep alone until she found it.

Cosima answered her ringing mobile phone and babbled in a torrent of Greek. Tally, who had attended evening classes in the language for several years, only to have her self-conscious efforts dismissed as 'an embarrassment' by her critical father, sealed her ears to the content of her half-sister's chatter, aware that the younger woman had assumed that she spoke no Greek at all.

The limo was purring down a wooded lane by the time that Cosima ceased chattering. She slid her phone back into her bag and shot Tally a guarded look. 'You know I'm not planning to tell my friends who you are. I'm sorry if that offends you but that's the way it is,' she declared. 'If Dad had wanted to acknowledge you as his daughter you would have been given his name. That you don't have our name says it all really.'

In response to that deeply wounding little announcement, Tally lost colour and before Cosima could add anything else, she said hurriedly, 'So, for your friends' benefit, who am I?'

'Well, obviously, you're still Tally Spencer, because that won't remind anyone of anything—I mean, these days people don't even remember Dad was ever engaged to anyone but *my* mother. But I certainly wouldn't want all that dirty washing brought out. I think it would be safest to say that you work for me.'

'In what capacity?' Tally enquired with a frown.

Cosima wrinkled her delicate little nose. 'You could say you're my personal assistant and that you do my shopping and look after invitations and things for me. Some of my friends have employees like that. You know you're only here in the first place because Dad said I couldn't come without you!' she complained petulantly.

Tally went red and nodded, her own quick temper surging, only to be suppressed by her common sense and intrinsic sense of tolerance for more volatile personalities. Cosima didn't intend to be rude or hurtful. She was simply rather spoilt and accustomed to being everyone's darling and she had not been taught to regard Tally as a real sibling.

'As an employee I'll be excluded from any activities and I won't be able to look out for you.'

'Why would I want you looking out for me?' Cosima asked her witheringly. 'You'll be totally out of your depth mixing with my friends.'

'I'll try hard not to get under your feet or embarrass you in any way but I did promise our father that I would take care of you and I like to keep my promises,' Tally retorted, tilting her chin and merely widening her fine eyes when her half-sister spat out a very rude word in challenging response. 'And if you're not prepared to let me try and do that, I might as well go home now—'

'What choice does that give me? Dad would be furious if I stayed here without you in tow. I can't believe we're related—you're so boringly stuffy, Tally!' Cosima hissed as the luxurious car came to a halt in front of a big Victorian mansion surrounded by acres of beautifully kept lawn. 'Isn't it ironic that you remind me of Dad?'

Tally said nothing, reluctant to fan the flames.

'You look like him as well,' Cosima slung in bitter addition, lashing out like the child she still was in so many ways. 'You've got his nose *and* you're small and chubby. Thank heaven *I* took after my mother!'

Chubby? Tally clenched her teeth on that cutting comment. She had the shape of an hourglass, full of breast and hip, but she had a tiny waist and did not have a weight problem. Did she look chubby? She winced. Small? Well, that was true. She was five feet two inches tall. Climbing out of the car, she watched her taller, slender half-sister greeting the leggy glamorous brunette at the imposing front door.

'Eleni Ziakis, our hostess. Tally Spencer, my personal assistant,' she announced chirpily.

A bunch of giggling young girls surged round Cosima in the echoing hall and it was left to Tally to follow the housekeeper upstairs. When Cosima joined them a moment later and saw Tally opening her weekend bag on one of the pair of single divan beds that furnished the bedroom, the younger woman turned to the housekeeper to say imperiously, 'I can't share a room with someone...I *never* share!'

An awkward few minutes followed while the older woman explained that all the guest rooms had already been allocated and Tally was forced to proclaim her willingness to sleep on bare boards if necessary. She was eventually shown up to another floor and put in a room already occupied by a member of the household staff who looked furious at the intrusion of a stranger. Taking the hint that her presence was unwelcome, Tally didn't bother taking the time to unpack and quickly removed herself again to rejoin her sibling.

As she walked along the corridor on Cosima's floor a tall broad-shouldered figure with a shock of damp spiky black hair appeared in a doorway. Unintentionally she froze and did a double take because the man wore only a towel wrapped round his lean brown hips. What wasn't covered by the towel was buff enough to make even Tally stare. He stood over six feet in height and enjoyed the wide shoulders, muscular chest and corrugated six-pack stomach of an athlete. He was, without a doubt, the most gorgeous-looking guy she had ever seen with sculpted cheekbones, skin the colour of dulled gold and a beautifully shaped sensual mouth. The fact that he needed a shave and that black stubble accentuated his stubborn jaw line merely enhanced his masculine sex appeal. Tally was startled to discover that she literally couldn't take her eyes off him.

'I've just flown in from abroad and I'm too hungry to wait for dinner. I'd like sandwiches and coffee,' he announced, brilliant dark golden eyes arrowing over her expectantly and lingering, for he instantly noticed that she was an exceptionally pretty girl, even if she wasn't quite in his usual style. 'Would that be possible?'

'I'm sure it would be, but…'

'I can't raise anyone on the house phone. I did try.' A scorching smile slashed his handsome mouth, lending him more charismatic pull than any guy with his already stunning looks required.

'I'm not on the staff here,' Tally told him gently.

'You're not?' Sander studied her and the longer he looked, the more he liked what he saw. She had a knockout quality of warmth and friendliness that he found hugely attractive.

Her mass of dark blonde corkscrew ringlets was very unusual. Her eyes were the colour of shamrocks, her nose was endearingly freckled and her lush sexy mouth looked as though it would be most at home laughing or smiling. Her skin was as flawless as newly whipped cream. She was very natural, not a word or a state he was used to attaching to the women he met, and that intrigued him. He could tell at a glance that she didn't take herself too seriously because no woman of his acquaintance would have been caught dead in her ordinary jeans and khaki T-shirt combo. On the other hand, those unprepossessing garments encased a very shapely figure that went in at all the right places and came out wonderfully generously in others. His hooded dark gaze rested appreciatively on the ripe swell of her breasts below the fine cotton top. He liked a woman to look like a woman, not a skinny boy.

Beneath that speculative appraisal, Tally was getting breathless. 'No, I'm not on the staff but I'm not exactly a guest either. I'm here to sort of

look after one of the younger guests.' Registering that her tongue was running on without the
guidance of her brain, she fell silent and coloured hotly at the way in which his attention was
locked onto her breasts. She hated it when men
did that but somehow when *he* did it, it sent an
arrow of heat shooting down into her pelvis and
her nipples tightened and stiffened uncomfortably inside her bra.

'Look, if I see a member of staff downstairs
I'll mention your request,' Tally assured him.

'I'm Sander Volakis,' he informed her lazily,
his keen eyes trained to her like a hawk on the
hunt. She was different and he, having recently
dispensed with his latest bed partner because
of her strident demands for his attention, was
definitely in the mood for something different in
the female line. Someone more low-key and less
spoiled, he reasoned, a woman who might appreciate his interest without endeavouring to turn
a casual affair into the romance of the century.
A woman who worked for a living in an ordinary capacity would make a refreshing change
from the celebrity beauties and models he usu-

ally dated. If she had no interest in achieving her fifteen minutes of fame, she might also be more trustworthy and less likely to flog the story of their affair to some mucky tabloid publication, he reasoned broodingly, for he loathed that kind of exposure in his private life.

Tally nodded, not recognising the name but liking the fracturing edge of the foreign accent that roughened his deep dark drawl.

'And you are?' he prompted, noting her lack of response to his name and encouraged by the tantalising suspicion that she might know nothing about him. No preset expectations would make for a more laid-back affair.

Tally blinked in surprise at the question. 'Tally...Tally Spencer.'

'And Tally is short for?'

People didn't usually bother to ask and with reluctance Tally admitted, inwardly squirming, 'Tallulah.'

Sander grinned, his amusement unhidden. 'Lysander,' he traded mockingly as he withdrew into his room again. 'What *were* our parents thinking of?'

So preoccupied was Tally after that tantalising encounter that she almost walked head first into a pillar on the imposing landing that lay several yards further on. Blinking rapidly to clear her head, she descended the stairs and laughed at the recollection of the way her brain had gone walkabout and she had gawped at him as if he had magically dropped down from the sky. Evidently she was more susceptible to a good-looking guy than she had ever had reason to suspect. She was less amused by the recollection of her body's hormonal reaction to him—that just embarrassed and irritated her. No man had ever made her feel silly and all hot and shivery in his presence before. Lysander Volakis, Greek, named for a Spartan general and built like one, her brain added with defiant force. She passed on his request for sandwiches to a maid passing through the hall.

Tally found Cosima in a girlie, giggly huddle in one corner of a gracious reception room and it didn't take her teenaged sister's warning look for Tally to decide that she was too mature to join the group without casting a dampener over their mood. There were drinks glasses on the table but there was no way of knowing who was drinking what in such a gathering. But Tally wondered anxiously if her sibling *was* consuming alcohol and if her father turned a blind eye to his daughter doing it a year short of the legal age limit. Determined not to get on the wrong side of her sister, however, she went off to explore the house and grounds.

Eleni Ziakis, his late brother's former fiancée, delivered Sander's sandwiches and coffee to his bedroom with her own fair hands and then she lingered as if her legs had turned to stone. Indeed so intent was the talkative brunette on ensuring his comfort, hanging on his every word and assuring him of how very welcome he was in her home, that she killed his appetite. It was steadily turning into the weekend from hell, Sander decided grimly when he finally saw her off. Eleni's parents were not present to act as hosts, there was a bunch of teenyboppers running about the place with Eleni's kid sister, Kyra, and Sander had walked into two of his ex-girlfriends within minutes of his arrival. One he was quite happy to catch up with, but the other—Birgit Marceau—was a less welcome sight. Birgit, the moody and tempestuous daughter of a French construction magnate, had taken their brief affair the year before way too seriously and had dealt badly with the break-up. Although Sander knew that he had done nothing wrong, he always felt uncomfortable when Birgit's limpid brown eyes followed him mournfully round the room.

Tally wiled away an hour or so exploring the grounds before she ended up at the stable block, meeting and greeting the various mounts. Offered the chance to ride a friendly mare the following morning, she had to pass because she had never learned. She would once she was earning enough money to cover lessons, she told herself firmly. Crystal had insisted on her daughter attending ballet classes that she hated for years, but had refused to allow a little girl she already saw as worryingly tomboyish take horse-riding lessons.

Having little interest in clothes, money and

men, Tally had not much in common with her mother. Her determination to live within her financial means and her dream of some day running her own interior design business were foreign to Crystal, who hated budgets and expected the man in her life to keep her. Tally's enthusiasm for life and new experiences and her sheer energy were equally strange to her indolent mother.

'Where have you been?' Cosima demanded when Tally walked back into the big front hall.

'Out seeing the horses,' Tally confided.

Drawing closer, Cosima wrinkled her dainty little nose with distaste. 'I can smell them on you!'

'I'll take a shower before dinner,' Tally said cheerfully and she headed for the stairs just as Sander strolled down them, looking impossibly cool in well cut chinos and an open shirt.

'Tally, you've been outdoors,' Sander noted, registering that her hair had been whipped into a gloriously wild tangle of streaming curls and her cheeks had been stung pink by the breeze. She looked more vibrant, sensual and kissable than ever. He loved the fact that she wasn't fussing with her appearance or trying to duck his notice because her appearance was less than perfect. He could not recall when a woman had last been so real in his radius and it was a powerful attractant.

'Saying hello to the horses,' Tally confided with her ready smile, colliding with dark golden eyes fringed by sooty black lashes and feeling positively dizzy. Close up he was absolutely breathtaking and her mouth ran dry and her knees felt weak.

'Maybe now that you've had a break you could take care of Cosima's ironing. I'm afraid the staff are very busy this evening,' another female voice interposed loudly.

Tally turned in some surprise to regard her hostess, Eleni Ziakis. 'I'm sorry but why would I do Cosima's ironing? I'm not her maid.'

'No, she's not,' Cosima was quick to agree, her discomfiture patent in the face of Tally's polite bewilderment.

Sander recognised with impatience that Eleni had spotted his interest in Tally and he strode off before his presence could trigger any further baiting from that source. Women, he thought in exasperation; can't live with them, can't live without them. His keen gaze was welded by libidinous male instinct to the voluptuous sway of Tally's beautifully rounded backside as she climbed the stairs and the ready pulse of arousal at his groin let him know that he had gone without sex long enough to be getting uncomfortable. Her exuberant smile had informed him, should he ever have doubted the fact, that his interest was reciprocated. He would not be sleeping alone that night, he decided hungrily.

'When the heck did you get to know Sander Volakis?' Cosima gasped in disbelief, curiosity having sent her upstairs in her half-sister's wake.

'I ran into him earlier and he introduced himself…it's no big deal,' Tally fielded lightly.

'The way Eleni was watching the two of you, it was a very big deal to her!' Cosima laughed. 'She used to be engaged to Sander's older brother, Titos, but he was killed in a car crash last winter. I think Eleni's trying to keep her interest in the family but she'll have her work cut out. Sander is a real womaniser!'

In the midst of struggling to conceal her interest in those titbits of information, Tally was betrayed into turning right round and saying, 'Is he?'

'He has a new woman every month. Don't waste your time, Tally,' Cosima warned her. 'Everybody dreams of pulling Sander but you'll never make the grade.'

Tally flushed, her freckles standing out clearly against her fair complexion. 'I have no desire to make the grade,' she lied, and the very fact that she knew she was lying affronted her as she had always believed that she had more sense than to be attracted to the sort of arrogant guy who scored women like goals on the football pitch and marked a notch his bed post accordingly.

'I'm not trying to put you down but you're *so* not his type. He goes for really beautiful women…models, actresses,' Cosima told her, her brown eyes scanning Tally's unconsciously disappointed face with a touch of condescending amusement. 'He's got quite a reputation…'

'I'm *not interested* in Sander Volakis!' Tally proclaimed in a tone of annoyance.

Cosima made no attempt to hide her amusement. 'Well, I wouldn't say no if I got the chance and Dad would back me all the way—Sander is what is known as "eligible", which basically means that the girl who gets him to the altar will have done very, very well for herself indeed!'

'I gather he's rich,' Tally remarked, irritating herself, for while pride made her want to drop the subject, the curiosity that needled her and drove her on was stronger still.

'I heard he made his first million before he even left school and even before you take his business interests into account you have to consider the family fortune,' Cosima responded in a suitably lowered tone, an avaricious gleam in her gaze. 'They made it in shipping and business is thriving.'

Tally actually found herself feeling sorry for Sander Volakis. Evidently his wealth and his family's made him a target for ambitious socialites and gold-diggers. It struck her as ironic that Cosima, who had never ever had to worry about the cost of anything, should be so very obsessed with what everyone was worth, but that was how it was. Her half-sister measured people and their importance purely in terms of cash and Tally was very much aware that her own lack of money increased her lowly status in Cosima's eyes.

However, when Cosima showed off her pathetically crumpled evening outfit Tally took pity on the younger girl. Cosima had never wielded an iron in her life but was forced to agree to try when Tally offered to teach her how it was done. For the first time Tally felt like a real sister and the two young women ended up in paroxysms of giggles over Cosima's clumsy amateurish efforts at the ironing board.

'What are you wearing?' Cosima finally thought to ask.

'Nothing very exciting.'

'I'd loan you something but…' Cosima glanced at their combined reflections in the wardrobe mirror and nothing more needed to be said. Cosima was tall and very slim while Tally was small and curvy. They would never be able to share clothes.

'I'm fine.' Tally was accustomed to such re-marks, having grown up in the shadow of her taller, thinner mother who had tried to put her on a diet at the age of nine. Binkie had had to utilise a lot of tact to persuade Crystal that no amount of dieting was likely to give Tally the same long lean lines as her mother.

She donned her dull black chain-store dress knowing that, in her sombre apparel, purchased purely because it was suitable for so many pur-poses, she would resemble a crow amongst a flock of exotic birds. For the first time she looked at her reflection and experienced a daunting pang of regret for attributes she did not have. What evil fate had given her corkscrew curls, freckles and breasts like melons instead of straight silky hair and petite feminine proportions? Binkie had tried to teach her charge that looks weren't important but Tally knew she lived in a world where appearance always counted. It mattered when you went for an interview and it mattered even more when you wanted to attract a man.

Did she really want to attract a wealthy wom-aniser? *Who are you trying to kid?* Tally scolded herself for being so silly and superficial all the way downstairs as she trailed in her effervescent teenaged sister's wake. She espied Sander at the far end of the table seated beside Eleni Ziakis, who wore an eye-catching white gown that bared one shoulder, and she tried not to take strength from the fact that he looked bored stiff. Cosima was no company at all while she giggled with her friends, exchanged confidential chat in whispered Greek and texted constantly on her phone. When the meal was over, it was announced that drinks would be served afterwards.

'I'm going to have an early night.' Cosima smothered a yawn with one hand and complained, 'I'm really sleepy and there's a big party here tomorrow.'

Tally was relieved to be released from her chaperoning duties. Thinking cheerfully about the paperback romance she had packed, she was crossing the hall towards the staircase when Sander intercepted her.

'Tally...'

Tally spun round and tipped her head back, dark blonde curls spiralling back from her cheekbones where the ready colour of awareness ignited the minute she met intent dark golden eyes. 'Yes?'

'Let's go out for a drink,' he suggested lazily, his attention roaming inexorably from her bright beautiful eyes down to her generous mouth and the voluptuous breasts shaped by her dress.

'I was thinking more of going to bed...' she began, tempted almost beyond bearing to say yes there and then. However, when she caught the amused gleam of confidence in his stunning gaze betraying his appreciation of her unintentional double entendre, she grasped the fact that he was expecting her to spend the night with him. As she turned cold at the suspicion that he saw her as a very sure thing in that respect, she glimpsed Eleni Ziakis staring coldly at them from a doorway and her colour heightened even more.

Her light 'Thanks but no thanks' tripped off her tongue without hesitation.

Startled by the kind of refusal that so rarely came his way, Sander stared down at her with a searching frown.

Awkward with the resulting silence, Tally felt prompted to fill it with a reasonable excuse and said, 'I've got a great book to read.'

Sander, glib of tongue though he was, had no answer for that and Tally, conscious of how silly that last comment had been and hot with mortification at her ineptitude, fled upstairs. Mercifully her reluctant room mate was nowhere to be seen and Tally climbed into bed with her book. The adventures of a heroine who seemed to attract an incredible number of different men, not one of whom she wanted, only irritated Tally and the mood she was now in and she put the book aside and doused the light. But sleep was not so easy to find, for her thoughts were running back and forth over Sander's brief invitation, and questioning why she had turned him down flat and in a way that would ensure he would never ask her again.

His approaching her when there were so many beautiful young alternatives available had shocked her. She knew she didn't fit in with the exclusive guests staying at Westwood Manor. She didn't have the right clothes, the right accent, background or attitude. So why had he selected her for his invitation? Could it have been because he assumed that she would be flattered, impressed to death and a pushover in the sex stakes? Or was that her low self-esteem doing the talking instead of her brain?

After all, a rich, sophisticated, good-looking guy had asked her out and she had said no because she was unprepared, and because deep down inside she was so insecure that she had felt he had to have an ulterior and base motive for choosing her. That was pathetic and most likely nonsense, she told herself impatiently, thoroughly irritated by the manner in which she had reacted. She fell asleep wishing she had said yes, wishing it over and over again…

Tally awoke a short time later with a start to find the light on and her room mate noisily rummaging through a drawer. She sat up blinking and, as she did so, her attention fell on a dainty vanity case sitting behind the door. Dismay filled her because it was a designer piece that belonged to Cosima; her half-sister was bound to be looking for it. Checking her watch and registering that it was only midnight, Tally got up, pulled on her robe and grabbed the case, planning to slide it just inside Cosima's bedroom on the floor below.

But when she gently opened the door a small way, she peered through the crack and saw the bedroom was still brightly lit and the bed unoccupied. Entering the room and setting the vanity case down on the dressing table, she noted that the bathroom was empty as well and she wondered where Cosima was. It was when she was walking back across the main landing that she thought she heard her sibling's voice and that it sounded oddly shrill. Approaching the banister, she looked down into the hall below.

She was astonished to see that the massive front door was standing wide and that Sander Volakis was guiding her swaying sister towards the stairs. My goodness, had they been out somewhere together? *I wouldn't say no if I got the chance*, her half-sister had admitted earlier. Had Cosima said yes where Tally had said no? But Tally had no time to consider those daunting questions as Cosima was noisily chattering in slurred and hiccuping Greek, her eye make-up smeared round her eyes and her short skirt rucked up to show too much thigh. It was clear that she had over-indulged in some substance and that, as a result, she could hardly walk. Appalled by what she was seeing, Tally hurried down the stairs to find out how the younger woman had got into such a state…

CHAPTER TWO

'WHAT on earth have you done to her?' Tally demanded angrily before she even reached the hall.

Sander Volakis shot her an outraged look from scorching golden eyes. 'This is not a conversation you and I are going to have...'

Tally folded her arms and blocked his path. 'I assure you that we are going to have that conversation, whether you want it or not. It looks as though Cosima's been drinking. Are you aware that she's only seventeen?'

'Aren't you the one who's supposed to be looking after her?' Sander slashed back in blatant condemnation. 'Tonight, you're doing a lousy job of it!'

Tally was mortified, her fair skin blossoming pink at that jibe, which hit her right where it hurt. Evidently Cosima had pulled the wool over her eyes earlier that evening by faking tiredness and assuring her that she was going straight to bed. Having got Tally off her case she had then, it seemed, gone out. With Sander? Something hideously raw and painful twisted inside Tally's stomach as she tried to deal with that unwelcome thought. Eleni Ziakis joined them, took in the situation at a glance and stared with a raised brow at Tally, making her writhingly aware that she was only wearing a wrinkled nightie and robe. As Eleni's kid sister appeared at her elbow, the brunette spoke quietly to her and then said, 'Kyra will take Cosima straight up to bed. Clearly she's been drinking. It's really not a good idea to attract attention to her condition by causing a scene, Miss Spencer—'

Tally compressed her full pink mouth. 'I wasn't aware that I was causing a scene. I would simply like to know what happened.'

'Cosima is in no fit state right now to tell you and I can assure you that her parents would prefer this matter to be kept private,' Eleni pointed out drily as Kyra took charge of Cosima and coaxed her carefully upstairs.

Sander thrust open a door on the other side of the hall. 'We'll discuss it in here, Tally.'

Tally knew that she was being challenged and she reckoned that he was so sharp he was in danger of cutting himself. She recognised the angry passionate glow in his gaze and the trace of aggressive colour accentuating the angles of his superb cheekbones. He had taken offence as only a guy unaccustomed to censure could do and she suspected that he was, at heart, the owner of a temperament as volatile as a smouldering volcano. And a trait that previously she loathed in her impulsive and often contrary mother suddenly became a deep and abiding source of fascination.

'This really isn't necessary, Sander,' Eleni Ziakis declared. 'There is no need for you to make any sort of explanation to anyone. Miss Spencer is being stupid and offensive.'

'I can handle this alone, thank you,' Sander fielded smoothly, ushering Tally past him and shutting the door in the brunette's face.

'Where did you take Cosima tonight?' Tally questioned shortly.

'I didn't take her anywhere. Why would I have?' A scornful dark brow elevated at the idea. 'To me, she's a little girl. I believe she and a group of her friends booked a taxi to take them to the pub in the village. When I arrived there the barman was refusing to serve Cosima any more alcohol without proof of ID. She had a blazing argument with him before stalking out in a temper.'

'Oh, for goodness' sake,' Tally groaned when he had finished speaking. 'She told me she was having an early night.'

'How many teenagers do you know?' Sander derided in disbelief. *An early night?*'

'All right, all right,' Tally sighed, feeling very foolish for being so trusting. 'So what happened after that?'

'I had one drink and left the pub about an hour later. Driving back I came upon Cosima sitting on a wall about a mile out of the village. She was so drunk she could barely stand and although I really didn't want to get involved I didn't feel that I could just leave her there. She got into my car and started crying hysterically—apparently she had arranged to meet her boyfriend at the pub but he didn't show up.'

Embarrassed colour was creeping up below Tally's skin, making her feel hot and uncomfortable. As she shifted position Sander focused fully on her and his attention could only linger on the magnificent expanse of the cleavage revealed by her open robe and low-necked nightie, the lace-decorated edge of which was gradually sliding apart and performing a very poor job of hiding her superb breasts, which were high and full and round. Just looking at that magnificent swell of feminine flesh, he got hard as steel.

'I had no idea Cosima had even gone out,' Tally admitted, sucking in a sustaining breath in the silence that suddenly seemed deafening.

'And if she did sneak out, you didn't want it to be with me,' Sander finished in shrewd silken addition.

At that crack, Tally literally froze as it hit her in the back like an unexpected bullet and left her reeling. For an instant she could not credit what he had dared to insinuate. 'I don't know what you're trying to say,' she framed, playing dumb with all her might.

'You know exactly what I'm saying. I was looking at you when you first saw me with Cosima,' Sander declared with supreme assurance, brilliant golden eyes astonishingly vivid below the heavy fringe of his black lashes. 'You didn't like it. You were angry with me more because you were jealous than because you thought I had been fooling around with Cosima!'

Tally went rigid, the colour in her cheeks seeping away as mortification crept through her like a freezing, debilitating fog. 'That is totally ridiculous. I hardly know you—why on earth would I be jealous?'

'You tell me.' As Sander voiced that invitation an insolent smile crept across his beautiful wilful mouth. And it *was* beautiful, she thought in almost pained recognition, as truly beautiful as he was altogether. He was an almost perfect masculine specimen, so gorgeous she couldn't stop looking and drinking him in like a life-enhancing elixir.

'I know enough about women to know what I read in your eyes, *glikia mou*,' he extended.

Her hands closed into tight angry fists. 'You didn't read anything in my eyes because there was nothing there to be read!'

'Liar...liar,' Sander rhymed smoothly and coolly enough to send a current of violent anger rushing through Tally's small still figure. For the very first time in her life she was mad enough at a man to want to hit him and to understand why provocation made people lose control. He might as well have tossed a hand grenade into the once tranquil pool of her mood, for all of a sudden she was on edge and ready to fight to defend her pride.

'You're incredibly vain,' Tally condemned furiously, watching him move closer with the same wariness with which she might have watched a lion strolling free of a cage. That lithe long-limbed grace of his simply enhanced his sex appeal so that in spite of her annoyance she found herself trapped into staring at him, studying his every move with an appetite for the visual that was new to her. 'I don't even like you.'

'I don't need you to like me,' Sander murmured, his perceptive dark scrutiny welded to her wide green eyes as he basked in the unwilling hunger he saw etched there. 'I only need you to want me.'

A prickling sensation touched the skin at the nape of Tally's neck as if that keen look of his had actually touched her. Part of her wanted to run away, but an even greater part wanted to see the moment out and cap his every comment. She had the vague spooky suspicion that someone was walking over her grave and that she was getting a wake-up call to finally experience that something she had waited so very long to find. She might want to slap him, she might want to shout at him and punish him for his exceedingly arrogant assumptions, but all of those very basic promptings were outrageously entangled with a very powerful desire for him to kiss her…and for her to *taste* him. He exuded a masculine strength that drew her even as it awakened her hostility. A pool of heat was forming low in her stomach while her bra was starting to feel like a metal restraint over the straining curves of her breasts.

'And you *do* want me,' Sander Volakis pronounced with confidence, dark eyes flaring to
hot gold as he searched her heart-shaped face
because, for a moment while she sparred with
him, he had wondered if just for once he could
have got it wrong. She had, after all, turned him
down when he'd asked her out earlier but now,
seeing that familiar look of desire in her gaze, he
was already wondering if that refusal could've
been a feminine ploy to spur his interest with a
false show of indifference. 'Just as I want you,
glikia mou.'

It was that roughened masculine admission that
slashed through Tally's angry defences like a cruelly efficient steel blade since, until that moment,
no man had ever contrived to make Tally feel
insanely attractive and sexy. But Sander Volakis
achieved that miracle at one stroke. While he
studied her with scorching intensity and with a
hunger he couldn't hide, excitement was lighting
her up inside like a fantastic firework display and
she smiled in delighted acknowledgement of an
appeal she had not known she had.

In receipt of that encouraging smile he pulled

her up against his lean, strongly built frame and brought his wide sensual mouth down on hers with demanding fervour. The skilled slide of his tongue between her parted lips sent a jolt of excruciating pleasure roaring through Tally like an electric shock but that initial sweetness was swiftly followed up by a fierce sense of unbearable craving. The kiss wasn't enough, nowhere near enough to meet the hunger that had fired her every skin cell with yearning. As she made an unconscious sound of dissatisfaction, her fingers dug tautly into his broad shoulders and she strained against the hard muscular contours of his broad chest and long, powerful thighs, urgently needing that physical contact to satisfy the tingling sensitivity of her nipples and the gnawing ache stirring between her legs.

In answer, Sander wrapped his arms round her and crushed her ripe mouth beneath his again, revelling in the taste of her and the lush firm softness of her shapely body against him. He wanted to gather her up and carry her off to bed to sate the fierce hunger she roused in him. He laced long fingers into the mass of her blonde curls and tipped her head back, meshing with glorious green eyes enhanced by skin the colour of clotted cream. Once again he attempted to pin-point the source of her powerful attraction. Was it the fearless honesty of those eyes, which met his with no hint of the coy suggestiveness and secrecy he was more accustomed to seeing? Or the wild sensuality with which she surrendered to his mouth and gave him back kiss for fiery kiss, stoking his desire to ever greater heights? In bed, he suspected, her passion would be a perfect spontaneous match for his own.

A mobile phone buzzed. Tally blinked like someone who having been hypnotised, was now being called back to awareness and immediately raised her hands to break free of his hold and step back from him, her sudden rigidity an in-stant rejection of the new intimacy they had es-tablished.

Perfectly attuned to her, Sander frowned as he switched his phone off. 'Don't be like that,' he groaned.

Tally was hot and dizzy. Dismayed to see that her robe was hanging open, she wrapped it more securely round her and reknotted the sash. Her hands were trembling and she was breathing rapidly, her bemused thoughts in freefall but that fast she understood that what he had just made her feel was the biggest temptation she had ever withstood. And she knew that what they had both felt was almost frighteningly powerful. Her nipples were tight, hard and almost stinging in response and at the heart of her she was uncomfortably hot and damp with a desire that clawed at her every sense. The taste of him? He tasted so unbelievably good that she could only want more…

Sander extended a lean brown hand. 'Come…'

'No, don't say it!' Tally urged, backing off another defensive step, feeling ridiculously like a woman in danger of losing her immortal soul. 'Goodnight, Sander.'

'You're not serious?' Sander breathed incredulously as she reached the door.

'Very serious.' Her hand closed tightly round the door knob and she refused to take the chance to turn her head and look at him again. 'I don't want anything else to happen.'

As the door swung shut on her quick exit Sander swore in raw and angry disbelief below his breath. What was the matter with her? Was the cut and run response her concept of flirtation? He had never ever got so hot with a woman only to have her walk away from him, leaving him unsatisfied. Nor had he ever been so surprised by the power of a woman to attract him. The prospect of a cold shower to cool his urgently aroused body had zero attraction.

Tally went to check on Cosima and found her sound asleep on top of the bed. Slipping off her half-sister's shoes, she arranged a throw over the younger girl and suppressed a sigh. She would not hold spite: tomorrow she would try harder to win Cosima's trust and perhaps she would get the chance to persuade her sibling that she was not sharing her weekend with some kind of prison warder.

But as Tally crept into the room she was sharing and slid back below the duvet on her bed, she was most troubled on her own behalf. When it came to the male sex she had always believed that she was intelligent and sensible and she had, if she was honest, looked down on several of the impulsive romantic choices her mother, Crystal, had made over the years. Yes, she acknowledged shamefacedly, she had felt quite superior in that field, convinced that she would never do anything half so foolish, so possibly she had deserved to be shot down in flames for being smug and short-sighted.

She had thought she knew it all and learned that in truth she was no more sophisticated than a toddler when it came to men. One salient fact had escaped her. Until she had actually experienced a genuinely powerful attraction to a man, she had not known what she was talking about. In the space of twenty-four hours, Sander Volakis had taught her things about herself that she really hadn't wanted to find out. Meeting Sander had proved to be a horribly humbling experience, she reflected ruefully. She had learned that just being near him could make her as giddy, hot and incapable of rational thought as an empty-headed adolescent. She had learned that she was human and fallible and capable of doing foolish things. She had also learned that refusing to give way to so strong a desire and practising self-denial could actually *hurt*.

Little wonder, then, that her mother had wrecked so many of her relationships by being unfaithful. Crystal Spencer had never said no to such an attraction when it came her way, had never put her current lover or indeed her child's stability ahead of sexual temptation. Crystal had done as she liked, when she liked, and had often paid the price for it. But Tally had also paid a high price too.

On more than one occasion, a young Tally had become attached to one of her mother's live-in boyfriends and that man's subsequent sudden disappearance from her life had distressed and confused her. At a tender age she had decided that men weren't reliable and that it was safer not to care for them. It was only when she was older, and with hindsight, that she'd had to admit it was her mother's behaviour that had often destroyed those relationships.

In any case, getting involved with Sander Volakis would lead nowhere. At least, it would have led her upstairs to his bedroom tonight, she admonished herself, well aware of his intentions. And deferred pleasure was definitely not something Sander knew much about. They had kissed and both had liked it and wanted more, and Sander would've seen no reason why they shouldn't immediately satisfy that desire. She had known exactly what was on his mind, had felt the urgency of his need against her and had recognised her own.

Maybe she was going to die a virgin, Tally thought in sudden horror, untouched by human hand and unwanted. Sander was too cool to chase her uphill and down dale in the hope that she might relent. Her sudden astounding desirability to a male of his looks and worldly status must just have been a fluke, one of those crazy inexplicable things.

Utterly crazy, she repeated doggedly to herself. They had nothing in common aside of the fact that she was Greek on her father's side and Sander didn't even know that because her father and his family were in no hurry to tell people who she was. She and Sander inhabited different worlds. By all accounts he was a wealthy high-flying businessman while she was a student. How much did she even share with Cosima who came from that same exclusive world of privilege? Precious little, she acknowledged sadly.

Yet, wasn't this supposed to be the stage of her life when she made mistakes and discovered who she really was? When she broke the rules and experimented? But jumping into bed with Sander Volakis would definitely be a big mistake. There would be no future with him and she would only get hurt. Did every relationship have to have a future? Did serious feelings always have to be involved? Was there no room for anything lighter and more temporary?

In her single bed, Tally tossed and turned and fought with herself. It wasn't as though she wanted to fall in love and get married any time soon. It wasn't as though she was daft enough to imagine that Sander even cherished any long-term intentions where she was concerned. Crystal Spencer's daughter could not be that naïve for, as a teenager, she had often been mortified to meet some strange man at the breakfast table while her mother flirted happily with her overnight guest, impervious to her daughter's embarrassment.

As it was dawn before Tally got to sleep, she awoke late. She was utterly disorientated when she was shaken to by Cosima the next day and discovered that it was already the afternoon.

'Oh, for goodness' sake,' she mumbled, pushing her tumbled curls off her brow and sitting up. 'How long have you been up?'

Her sibling was infuriatingly bright-eyed and bushy-tailed for a young woman who had gone to bed under the influence of alcohol. 'Long enough to play a couple of games of tennis this morning and then have lunch. Now the men are off on a shoot and we're going shopping, so you had better get up—'

'Shopping? Why?' Tally responded, pushing back the duvet.

'That question says it all, Tally. There is no such thing as *why* when it comes to shopping!' Cosima told her. 'There's a big party here tonight and you can't possibly wear that cheap LBD again, and I want something new as well.'

'About last night...' Tally began awkwardly.

'Don't preach,' Cosima urged with a steely look. 'But I do owe you an apology for this room—it's a dive.'

Tally absorbed the younger woman's grimace at the faded walls and worn furniture deemed suitable for staff rather than guests and laughed. 'It's not that bad. What happened to Chaz last night?'

Cosima stiffened defensively at that question about her boyfriend. 'He didn't turn up because he couldn't—he got lost,' she said with an air of defiance that suggested that some of her friends might already have been less than impressed by that excuse.

Tally found herself being hustled out of the mansion and into a customised Range Rover that belonged to one of her sister's friends. As she had not had the chance to have anything to eat her stomach was growling with hunger. During the drive back to London she tried to get Cosima to talk about Chaz but her sibling was disappointingly reluctant to part with any information.

Westgrave Manor was buzzing with bustling staff and caterers when Tally returned in a cab, the other girls having kept late beauticians' appointments at the local spa. Her father phoned and asked how the weekend was going. Tally told no tales but she did take the opportunity to ask what he had against her sister's boyfriend.

'Charles Roberts has drug convictions. He's an unscrupulous character and I don't want him anywhere near my daughter,' Anatole Karydas admitted grimly.

Tally made use of Cosima's en-suite bathroom as she had been told to do, showering and washing and drying her hair. This afternoon had been fun. Her sibling had insisted on buying her a new dress and, although the turquoise satin mini dress with the bejewelled neckline had a shorter hemline than Tally usually wore, she felt amazing in it, loving the bright zingy colour and the way it seemed to light up her face. She had no idea what it had cost and had no intention of asking. Sometimes she felt aged by the lowering awareness that she was generally more sensible than her mother and just for once she wanted to feel young and carefree without sweating the serious stuff.

Dinner was served as a buffet. Starving as she was, Tally helped herself to food and then when she saw Sander's proud dark head from a distance she abandoned that plate lest he think she was a greedy pig and filled another plate with a more sparing selection. Like lightning, she felt the excitement of him even being in the same room and she could barely credit the immaturity of her reactions, but her heart was already beating so fast and so violently it felt as though it were lodged at the foot of her throat and she couldn't eat.

A dark-haired young man smiled down at her and pressed a moisture-beaded glass into her hand. 'Have some champagne. I don't think we've met,' he murmured pleasantly. 'I'm Robert Miller...'

'Tally Spencer...gosh, this is awkward.' She laughed, struggling to maintain a grip on the glass, the plate and the cutlery, not to mention the evening bag dangling on her wrist.

He took the plate for her and urged her over to a table.

A surge of dark fury rippling through him

and sending golden sparks flaring in his dark eyes, Sander watched the whizz-kid software designer, Robert Miller, moving in on Tally. She *did* look incredibly sexy in her turquoise dress, its jewelled neckline seductively showcasing the creamy upper slopes of her breasts while the hemline showed off a good deal more of her shapely legs than had been on display the night before. The tightening swelling at his groin set his even white teeth on edge because he usually enjoyed a firmer hold on his libido.

As Cosima moved past, clinging to the arm of a tall man with dirty-blond hair spiked up, Tally called her name. Her sibling came to a reluctant halt to perform an introduction. While Cosima announced that her boyfriend had a booking at a fashionable club later that evening, Tally was instantly wary of Chaz, with his calculating blue eyes and tight controlling grip on the younger woman. At least thirty years of age, he was much older than she had expected and far too mature for a seventeen-year-old, she thought worriedly.

'I'll be leaving with Chaz soon to go to the club and I probably won't bother coming back here,' the teenager spelt out. 'But you mustn't tell Dad...'

Her heart sinking, Tally lifted her chin. 'I won't lie to him, Cosima.'

Angry resentment blazed in her sibling's eyes. 'But you *have* to—'

'I don't have to do anything,' Tally responded with gentle regret. 'And neither do you. I think you should finish out the weekend here with your friends.'

The younger woman hissed something very rude and stalked away. Wincing, Tally turned back to her companion. 'Sorry about that, but I'm supposed to be looking after her.'

'I suspect she's quite a handful,' Robert remarked with the wry smile of a man able to take a smart-mouthed teenager very much in his stride, pulling out a chair for her to sit down. 'Anatole Karydas' kid, isn't she? Do you work for him?'

Uncomfortable with that pretence insisted on by Cosima, Tally half turned her head away. 'Sort of...'

The passage of her uneasy gaze screamed to a

halt on Sander, who was watching her from the other side of the room. One glimpse of his lean, darkly handsome features made her gulp, drove her mind blank. Even at that distance his beautiful dark deep-set eyes could make her shiver with helpless awareness and tug her nipples into stinging tightness below her clothing. She had never felt like that before and the tingling pool of warm dampness gathering low in her body fascinated her as he awakened her sexuality as no other man ever had.

A waiter approached her with a glass on the tray. 'Miss Karydas sent it over with her compliments.'

'Oh…' Tally skimmed a brief glance at the fancy colourful cocktail and looked around for her sibling but couldn't see her. Was this Cosima's way of apologising? The glass was set down in front of her.

'If you don't eat your food will get cold,' Robert Miller drawled.

Dragging her attention from Sander Volakis demanded every atom of self-discipline Tally possessed. She *loved* to look at him and the temptation to stare at the sculpted masculine perfection of his face pulled at her with embarrassing persistence. She sat down, glanced at the food and realised her appetite had vanished. She took an exploratory sip of the drink she had been sent instead. It was very fruity and much more to her taste than alcohol usually was.

'Tally...' Sander murmured, casting a long dark shadow over the table with his brooding stance. 'Robert...'

Glancing up to encounter shimmering golden eyes and sensing the angry dissatisfaction he was struggling to hide in the set quality of his smile and his clenched fingers, Tally began to stand up. It was a visceral reaction to the unspoken emotional demand in his gaze and her immediate awareness that he did not like seeing her in another man's company. *Sander was jealous.* No man had ever been possessive of Tally before and, although for the first time in her life she was feeling her power as a woman, she discovered that she had not the smallest desire to use it on him.

Besides, the volatile flash of the hot-blooded

temperament he could not hide thrilled and fascinated her. Eleni Ziakis joined them and began to make determined conversation. In the midst of it Sander boldly closed his hand over Tally's to tug her out from behind the table. Only pausing to throw Robert an apologetic glance, Tally grabbed her colourful drink and made no objection to Sander closing an arm round her to lock her against his lean, powerful body in a demonstration that lit annoyance in Eleni's dark eyes. Tally ignored the other woman. Retrieved by Sander and momentarily mentally engaged in reliving the demanding urgency of his mouth on hers the night before, Tally was supremely happy but ever so slightly dizzy.

'Tonight you're with me,' Sander informed her darkly as he walked her away.

'And tomorrow?' Tally dared, snatching a thirst-quenching gulp of her drink.

Sander paused, looked down at her and lifted a lean brown hand to push a handful of blonde-coloured corkscrew curls behind one small ear in a confident caressing movement. His scorching golden eyes were welded to her heart-shaped face and she could not have broken free of that hold had her life depended on it. 'Tomorrow you'll still be with me, *glikia mou*,' he asserted, his other hand closing to her hip to urge her small curvy body closer to his.

And even through their clothing she could feel the long hard ridge of his erection and a dark forbidden excitement gripped her then.

'What are you drinking?' Sander prompted huskily.

'I don't know…Cosima sent it over. I was surprised because we'd had a disagreement and she was annoyed with me.' Tally frowned a little because she could hear her words slurring.

'What did you disagree about?'

'She wanted to leave with her boyfriend and I said I wouldn't cover up for her with her father. The boyfriend has drug convictions,' she whispered thickly, her tongue feeling too large for her mouth and bumping into her teeth.

'Let me get you something to eat,' he urged.

'Not hungry…in fact I feel a bit weird,' Tally confided, because her lower limbs felt oddly detached from the rest of her body and clumsy and it was taking major effort to get her lips and her tongue to frame words properly.

'How much have you had to drink?'

'Only this one...I *swear*,' she added vehemently when he sent her a suspicious look. 'I can't believe that I'm feeling like this after just one drink...'

Clutching his arm to steady herself on her jellied legs, she was relieved when he slotted her in behind a table and she could give up the struggle to stand upright. Her head felt too heavy for her neck and she propped her chin up on her upturned hand. She felt awful and could feel the world around her fading and closing in round her. 'Sander...I'm so sorry...I think I'm going to pass out...'

As she began to slump Sander signalled Cosima, who was watching them fixedly. He lifted the glass. 'Do I give this to the police?'

'The police?' Tally struggled to sit up again, mumbling in shock.

'The *police*?' Cosima squealed in horror.

'You spiked Tally's drink—'

'No...police...' Tally managed to frame with

dogged emphasis, catching a glimpse of her sibling's stricken guilty face. *'No police.'*

'Was she getting in the way of your fun? Well,
you just got in the way of mine!' Sander completed harshly as Tally slumped down on her
forearms on the table top. 'Not a good idea,
Cosima. Now you have to tell me what was put
in that drink and I'll decide what to do next.
Meanwhile the boyfriend leaves. Eleni doesn't
want anyone spiking drinks at her party.'

Cosima was watching Sander as a snake
watched a snake charmer and fright and fury
were warring for top billing on her lovely face.
Tally blinked drowsily and then finally closed
her weighted eyes in relief. Not even a fire alarm
could have roused her from her comatose state…

CHAPTER THREE

TALLY felt wonderfully comfortable as she opened her eyes slowly to focus on the elaborately gathered oyster silk canopy above her...

Propelled by sudden alarm, she sat up with a start, her widened eyes scanning her unfamiliar surroundings in dismay. This was not the bedroom she had been allotted. Morning light was seeping round the edges of the drapes and illuminating the opulent contours of a big room furnished with antiques. This was not Cosima's room, either. Her attention fell on the masculine clothing draped on a nearby chair and her attention immediately shot to her own body below the sheets. Finding her bra and pants still in place, she winced when she recognised the turquoise dress she had worn the night before lying on the floor in a heap with her shoes and evening bag.

Her last memories of the party came flooding back, before she noticed the fact that the pillow beside hers bore an imprint and heard the unmistakeable sound of water running beyond the door that was ajar at the far side of the bed. A door that led to an en-suite bathroom?

Tally was disconcerted and wired with consternation when Sander Volakis, his lean bronzed features extraordinarily handsome, strolled into the bedroom with only a towel anchored round his lean hips. He looked amazing, from his wide brown shoulders to the corrugated flatness of his stomach and long powerful legs. 'Ah…you're awake,' he pronounced in the most incredibly calm greeting.

Hugging the sheet to her throat, Tally viewed him furiously over the edge of it. 'How on earth did I get here? What happened? Did you sleep here last night as well?'

'Naturally, this is my room,' Sander supplied lazily.

'So what am I doing here?'

'There was nobody else to take on the job of

looking after you. After the doctor had checked you over—'

'The doctor?' Tally gasped, becoming suddenly ludicrously aware that her hair was probably standing on end and her make-up smeared all over her face. Her most pressing desire then was to leap under the bed and hide but she was forced to sit there, the squirming focus of his uncomfortably steady scrutiny. 'What doctor?'

'Eleni and I thought it best to have the local GP check you out in case it was necessary for you to go to hospital. Cosima swore that she only put a sleeping pill—which she got from a friend, *not* the boyfriend according to her,' Sander explained drily. 'The GP asked for the bottle, consulted a colleague by phone and decided you were unlikely to suffer any lasting harm. He then gave Cosima a lecture about the risks of giving unprescribed drugs to third parties that left her in hysterics.'

'Oh, for goodness' sake,' Tally groaned, cringing at the amount of fuss and drama her passing out had caused. But she was genuinely disturbed that her sibling had subjected her to such a dangerous experiment and resolved to have a serious talk with the younger woman. However, at that moment she had a more pressing cause for concern: the presence of her underwear suggested that nothing intimate had occurred between her and Sander but she wanted to be sure. 'I gather that…er…we didn't do anything last night?' she prompted, her cheeks reddening fierily.

'I like my women awake,' Sander asserted. 'Awake, lively and consenting. I would never take advantage of a woman while she was helpless.'

'I'm sorry. I didn't mean to insult you but I still don't understand why I seem to have spent the night in your room…'

'Cosima didn't volunteer to assist you and I chose not to leave you in the hands of the staff. None of them knew you. I wanted to be sure you were all right.'

'Thanks.' Unable to sit there any longer when she needed to use the bathroom, Tally wriggled out from below the sheet, hurried round the foot of the bed and sped for the bathroom like a runner sprinting for the finishing line.

Happily engaged in enjoying the view of her lush breasts and bottom bouncing in the inadequate support of a skimpy black bra and knickers, Sander just laughed as the door shut behind her. He loved her small but wonderfully curvaceous body and she was shy, which he was even less accustomed to. Shy, possibly even a little prudish, which would be an even more unfamiliar female trait for him, he acknowledged wryly, since the women he usually shared a bed with thought nothing of nudity. He'd had to have a very cold shower in the middle of the night to douse the flames of arousal caused by Tally cuddling her half-naked curves up against him.

Tally loosed a moan of horror at her tousled reflection in the many mirrors surrounding her. It was the bathroom from hell, she decided, unnerved by the number of reflections hitting her from every angle. Grabbing up a masculine comb, she began to enforce order on her curls while striving to discourage the frizz factor. After washing her face and making use of one of the new toothbrushes on offer, she stepped into the shower. She was still embarrassed by the gauche manner in which she had fled from the bedroom.

After all, in the circumstances, Sander Volakis had behaved surprisingly well for a male with the reputation of a rich, spoilt womaniser. Although he hardly knew her and their relationship only encompassed a passionate kiss or two, last night when it mattered he had looked out for her and looked after her. A lot of blokes would just have turned their backs and walked away from so awkward a scenario. That he hadn't taken the easy way out really impressed her.

Donning the white towelling robe on the back of the door, Tally pushed her underwear into the pocket and returned to the bedroom.

'Breakfast?' Sander asked lightly, straightening from the table by the window, which was spread with a selection of food. Clad only in a pair of soft blue denim jeans that moulded his narrow hips and long powerful thighs and a white tee, he was a heartstoppingly attractive figure.

'No, thanks, I'd better get back to my room.'

'Why do you always want to run away from

me?' Sander enquired, ebony brows drawing together above his stunning eyes in a frown.

Tally recognised in a thought that was not for sharing that the more he made her feel, the more he scared her, and the more her native caution urged her to keep her distance. Sander Volakis was dangerous to her peace of mind, to everything she had ever known about herself, because with him she wanted to throw away the rule book and stop playing safe. She only had to look at him to want to walk into his arms and touch him, so retreat struck her as the wiser part of valour.

'I'm not running away,' she proclaimed with a taut smile.

As poised as a lion ready to spring, Sander paced several steps closer. 'You feel the same vibe that I do.'

It was true, because when he was that close she was so tense she could hardly breathe, and when he reached for her and drew her close by dint of closing his hands round the ends of the sash tied round her waist she made no objection; indeed she laughed with a playful sense of freedom that was new to her.

'I want you, *moli mou*,' he growled soft and low, the roughened edges of his fracturing accent purring sexily along the vowel sounds.

'You can't have me,' she told him daringly.

'Just one little taste before you go,' Sander husked, holding her against him and then lowering his arrogant dark head to toy with her full pink lips in a slow sensual assault.

As he suckled at her full lower lip his breath fanned her cheek and she shivered. A split second later as he deepened the pressure her pulses leapt like trapeze artists on a high wire, her mouth opening for the plundering pillage of his tongue, excitement hurtling through her in a shower of energising sexual sparks. It was more than a taste, it was a feast, as a sure masculine hand closed round the swelling softness of a rounded breast, his thumb grazing the swollen tender tip so that she gasped below his mouth, every sense greedily scrambling to get the most out of every new sensation. Go, her mind echoed in a curious refrain. Go...*where*? Just then she didn't want to go anywhere if it meant separating from him.

Sander hauled her right off her feet and up

into his arms and kissed her with stimulating thoroughness. The arm he banded across her hips pressed her into revealing contact with his potent arousal. By the time that he brought her down on the bed with him excitement was racing through Tally at the speed of a runaway train. She had an out-of-control sensation that should have scared her but instead she felt elated as she revelled in the heightened responses of her body and the sense of rightness between them. He felt like the guy she had long been secretly hoping to meet and, while a little voice at the back of her mind warned her that she had only just met him, he had already won her trust by taking care of her the night before. And trust was everything to Tally.

'You have gorgeous breasts, *glikia mou*,' Sander husked, the robe pushed apart to reveal the pouting globes he was shaping in his palms, long brown fingers tugging at her protuberant nipples in a tantalising caress. 'I've been fantasising about them since we first met…'

Colour washed up over her face, her green eyes very bright, for she did not know what to say and she was hugely uncomfortable with the sight of her bare flesh in the daylight flooding through the windows. But before she could react, Sander bent his proud head to catch a tender rose-coloured tip between his lips and lave it with his tongue and a ball of heat burst in her pelvis, spreading aftershocks of stimulation through her entire lower body. For the first time in Tally's life, desire was rippling through her in mindless waves and she could not believe how powerful and tenacious a hold it had on her. He kissed her again hard and fast and she stopped thinking altogether, her hands smoothing restively over the satin skin of his broad shoulders and her fingers spreading against the hair-roughened breadth of his chest. The husky soapy scent of him fresh from the shower was an aphrodisiac.

'Are you staying?' Sander prompted thickly, his accent scissoring sexily along the syllables.

For an instant, breathless and with her body on a high of burning desire, she could not fathom why he should be asking her such a question.

Sander ran a teasing fingertip along her reddened lower lip. 'I want you. I wanted you the first moment I saw you but I like to play fair. I also want your assurance that you're fully recovered from last night.'

'Of course I am.' *I wanted you the first moment I saw you*; yes, she liked the sound of that, as it so perfectly matched the way she had felt when she first saw him. The wanting, the burning craving, had been as instantaneous for her as a chemical reaction. She gazed up into lustrous dark eyes shaded with gold in the light and her heartbeat thudded heavily, the muscles in her pelvis clenching in a response that came as easily as the next breath to her lungs. But that insane pulse of desire pulling at her made it almost impossible for her to think clearly. Was she going to sleep with him? She wanted to. She knew that with a little thought she could probably come up with at least twenty reasons why she should not sleep with him but, just for once, Tally was rebelling against her cautious and sensible side. Sander was beautiful, sexy and surprisingly thoughtful and she was flattered that he found her so attractive. She was convinced that she would never find a more suitable male to be her first lover.

'Tally...' Sander smiled down at her.

And because she already feared that she was thinking too much and detracting from her newly found confidence and spontaneity, she pulled him down to her and kissed him with all the fierce passion she had always suppressed.

Sander was blown away by her enthusiasm: she was like a torch in his arms and she had the body of a goddess. He traced the swollen heart of her and found her flatteringly wet and ready for the next step. He rolled on a condom with practised ease and without any further ado, for he was hugely aroused, he pulled her under him and pressed back her knees.

As eager as he was for the final act, the pulse of desire in her pelvis steeping up in urgency, Tally made no demur. But as she felt the sure probe of his manhood at her entrance, nerves made her suddenly tense and his thrust when it came pierced her deep and hurt. At the sound of her cry of pain and resulting grimace, Sander had to struggle to rise above the pleasure of the tight grip of her inner muscles. Momentarily he froze and swore, pulling back from her in an abrupt motion.

'What the hell…?' Sander exclaimed.

Gripped by severe embarrassment when she realised how he had reacted to her cry, Tally breathed, 'You didn't have to stop.'

Sander frowned down at her as though she was talking in another language. 'Of course I did. I hurt you.'

Tally could feel herself reddening so hotly that she felt as if she were roasting alive from outside in. 'I didn't realise it would be so…er…uncomfortable the first time,' she mumbled apologetically.

As Sander retreated even further from her he noticed a spot of blood on the white fibres of the robe she lay on. 'The first time? Are you saying that you were a virgin?'

Tally focused on a strong brown and very tense shoulder. 'Er…yes.'

Sander rolled all the way back from her and sprang off the bed in one defensive movement.

'So what's your game?' he demanded before he disappeared into the bathroom.

'I beg your pardon?' Confused, Tally hastily flipped the robe back across her exposed body and sat up, wincing at the tenderness between her thighs. She was totally mortified by the ignominious ending to their intimacy. He had stopped dead, clearly had had no desire to continue and he was angry as well. Having always assumed that men found it a challenge to stop at the eleventh hour, as it were, she was bewildered and inclined to think that she must have turned him right off.

Sander reappeared and scooped up his boxers to pull them on. He sent her a scorching glance of suspicion from stunning dark golden eyes. 'What are you playing at? You're a virgin. I didn't sign up for complications.'

Although she wanted to sink through the mattress, Tally, in her turn was becoming angry at his attitude. 'What's *your* problem? Perhaps I should've warned you—'

'Of course you should've warned me!' Sander blasted back at her, his lean dark face grim. 'If

I'd known I would have taken my time and I wouldn't have hurt you!'

Her cheeks red, Tally tied the sash on her robe and slid off the bed onto nerveless lower limbs. 'Well, let's not make a meal of it. I appreciate that you're surprised but I don't think there's any reason for you to be so annoyed with me.'

'I don't like surprises. Women usually have an agenda with me...'

Tally pulled a face as she stooped hurriedly to gather up her dress and shoes. 'Could my agenda be...getting away from you as quickly as possible?' she prompted dulcetly, fighting her sense of humiliation with all her might.

'Women don't usually sacrifice their virginity in a casual encounter.'

'Well, that's me told, is it?' Tally quipped, paling at that description of their intimacy. 'Sorry if I departed from the norm and spooked you. I didn't realise that you only dallied with identikit females. What sort of women are you used to? Or is that a rude question?'

Sander could not recall when he had last met a woman who could have equalled Tally

Spencer's innocence. Even when he was a teenager his female companions had been as sophisticated and nonchalant about sex as he was himself. In the world in which he moved everyone was sexually experienced and it had not even crossed his mind, in spite of the shyness he had noticed, that she might be any different.

'You're my very first virgin,' Sander admitted, zipping his jeans, and surveyed her with brooding tension. 'I've heard that the less experienced a woman is, the more she expects from a man.'

'You heard wrong, where I'm concerned anyway. I may have almost zero experience but I expect nothing from you, least of all a lecture about sacrificing my virginity in a casual encounter!' Tally traded flatly, tilting her chin, corkscrew curls shimmying back from her flushed cheekbones, enhancing the bright green colour of her eyes.

'I wouldn't have chosen to make love to you if I'd known I would be your first lover. You must've had some reason for waiting so long to have sex...'

Tally flinched, determined not to stroke his

ego by admitting that it had taken him to fill her with the desire and need to experience that ultimate intimacy. 'I'm not exactly an old lady. Nor am I as unusual as you think. Not every girl sleeps around from a young age. The time just felt right.'

'But why did you pick me? Or is that a stupid question?' Sander enquired cynically.

'A stupid question?' Tally queried from the bathroom doorway, because she was planning on getting dressed but not in front of him.

'Maybe working for the Karydas girl has given you a taste for her lifestyle and you're hoping that I will deliver it,' Sander derided.

'Oh, so now you think I'm a gold-digger...my goodness, you're as obsessed with your financial worth as Cosima is!' Tally condemned furiously, outraged by his suspicions about her character. 'Get a life, Sander! We had sex but I'm not expecting a commitment of any kind from you! In fact if I ever see you again after this fiasco, it will be too soon!'

Within minutes, Tally had shed the robe and donned her clothing. She emerged from the bathroom again and pushed forcefully past Sander, who was in her path, by raising her hands to push against his broad chest in vehement rejection.

'Tally—'

'Get lost!' Tally launched back at him angrily as she stalked out of the room and headed straight upstairs to her own.

So much for him being the special guy whom she was connecting with, she castigated herself bitterly while she eradicated all evidence that she had not spent the night in her own bed. Having donned casual clothing and packed her stuff for departure, suddenly she could not wait to go home and she took out her mobile phone to check out the local train times and then to ring her father. It was not a call she enjoyed making but she felt that it was only fair to tell him what had happened, lest he receive some other version of the truth from his daughter. Anatole Karydas was shocked and rather silent and it was with a heavy heart that she finally went downstairs to confront her sister.

'Oh, it's you…' Wrapped in a colourful silk kimono, Cosima pulled a long-suffering face and reluctantly let her into her bedroom. 'I suppose you're expecting me to grovel but you should've minded your own business last night. Even though Chaz had nothing to do with what happened, he was thrown out of the party. No doubt you're pleased about that!'

'Right at this minute, I couldn't care less about you or your boyfriend. Thanks to you, I passed out in public and was left to depend on the kindness of strangers while I was unconscious,' Tally reminded the younger woman, her bright eyes level and accusing, her hurt over Cosima's lack of concern or guilt on that score well concealed because she had her pride. 'How could you put me through that? It was a very dangerous thing to do and a very unpleasant experience.'

Cosima was defiant. *'So?'* she traded sulkily. 'I didn't want you here this weekend.'

'It won't be a problem you have again,' Tally assured her drily. 'I'll see you…or maybe I won't.'

Her sibling followed her to the door, only then noting the small case Tally had left in the corridor. 'Where are you going?'

'I have a train to catch—'

'But you're supposed to be leaving with me this afternoon,' the pretty brunette protested, her surprise and annoyance patent.

'I'd like to go home now. All the best, Cosima,' Tally pronounced with sincerity and departed in relief...

CHAPTER FOUR

HAVING breakfasted, Sander was just settling down with the financial section from one of the Sunday broadsheets when he glanced out of the window and saw Tally's small figure wheeling a case at a brisk pace down the driveway.

Thinking about what might have prompted her sudden departure from Westgrave Manor, Sander's lean powerful body became tense and he stifled a curse. It was nothing to do with him if that spoilt little shrew, Cosima, had sacked her assistant. But, a moment later, prompted by the same instincts that had once made him search night and day for a week to find a lost dog, Sander sprang upright with a frown and headed out to his car.

It was not that he regretted what he had said to Tally Spencer—he did not. Given a choice he would never have chosen to sleep with a virgin. It was not even that he was still interested in her—he was not. Sander liked sex to be simple and his very frustrating encounter with Tally had persuaded him that in straying from his usual female format he had made a cardinal error. Instead of experiencing a refreshing difference and a lot of passion with his choice of an 'ordinary' girl as a lover, he had landed a virgin and a feisty and ungrateful one at that. A fast learner as he was, he knew that in future he would stick to the experienced sophisticates he was accustomed to.

Tally glanced up when she heard the growling sports car behind her slow down, but when she saw Sander gazing back at her from the lowered driver's window, colour stung her cheeks and her chin came up at a defensive angle. 'What do you want?'

Her dark blonde hair was blowing in the breeze in a spectacular torrent of curls. Her vivid green eyes were wide and defensive above her creamy skin and her soft full lips that had tasted like ripe strawberries were slightly open and moist. The familiar surging heaviness of reaction at his groin infuriated Sander and he studied her with frowning force, wondering what it was about her that got to him sexually every single time.

'I'll give you a lift to wherever you're going,' he told her.

'Thanks, but I'm heading to the station and it's only down the road,' Tally told him stonily, convinced as she was that he could only have followed her because he felt sorry for her.

Those lean bronzed features of his were so breathtakingly handsome that that embarrassing need to look and then look again at him was already assailing her afresh. He levelled dark golden eyes fringed by silky black lashes as long as fly-swats on her and she wanted to scream. She'd had sex with him and although the act had not reached the usual conclusion it had still proved a disaster. That awareness clawed at her, making her eyes evasive and her spine rigid as discomfiture spread through her like toxic waste that suppressed every warmer response.

Sander climbed out as if she hadn't spoken and snatched up the small case by her side to shove it into the small space behind the front seats. 'Come on,' he urged impatiently.

Unprepared to have a stand-up row with him within sight of the manor house, Tally compressed her generous mouth and slid into the passenger seat, feeling hugely self-conscious and uncomfortable.

'Did the spoiled brat sack you?' Sander enquired, accelerating down the drive. He was striving not to notice the way that her fine wool sweater hugged her breasts and the tight denim defined her rounded thighs, or to recall that glorious body spread before him naked in an invitation that had gone badly wrong.

'Er...no. We just decided to go our separate ways sooner rather than later,' Tally parried, not wanting to tell lies or to brand Cosima a liar. She felt uneasy about this fact, yet to tell him the truth was impossible. He was Greek born and bred like her sibling and he moved in the same social circles, so she was too proud to admit her real relationship to Cosima when her father and his family preferred to virtually ignore her existence.

'That kid is out of control. She committed an offence last night,' Sander pointed out as he drove out onto the main road.

'She's young and wilful. No doubt she'll get over it—'

'What age are you?' he cut in abruptly.

'Twenty.'

'You come across as more mature than that.' Sander was surprised and not best pleased by the news that she was only just out of her teens.

'Just not mature enough to head you off this morning!' Tally rejoined with scantily leashed bitterness.

'Don't take it that way,' Sander drawled, shooting a measuring glance at her strained profile as he parked on the quiet road outside the train station.

Tally shot him a look of naked loathing. 'How did you expect me to take it? It was a lousy experience and you insulted me into the bargain!'

In the simmering silence, Tally scrambled out and flipped round to reach for her case but Sander was faster. Colour scoring his high cheekbones at the bite of that word, 'lousy', and the unexpected force of her antipathy, he lifted her case out and extended his arm to her in silence at the front of the car. His self-command in the face of her emotional outburst tightened her expressive mouth and made her feel foolish.

As she stood there rigid with the force of aggression she was containing and with her luminous eyes still hurling angry defiance, Sander was amused and intrigued. Women never fought with him and even more rarely criticised him and she did not look the type to do so either, for she was so small and softly rounded in shape, an exceedingly feminine woman in appearance. Was it that quality that encapsulated her appeal for him? He was tempted to haul her into his arms, lift her up against him and prove that he could turn 'lousy' into orgasmic delight and it annoyed him that he was not to have that opportunity.

'We should meet for dinner some evening,' Sander murmured silkily.

'You've got to be joking!' Tally slung, turning on her heel to walk away without even a hint of hesitation.

'You don't know what you're missing, *glikia mou*.'

'Don't I? I told you how I felt about you!' she tossed back sharply. 'And don't call me your sweetheart. I'm not your sweet anything!'

'These are absolutely beautiful!' Binkie exclaimed, burying her nose in the fragrant bouquet of roses that had just been delivered.

'My goodness,' Tally remarked, joining her in the kitchen. 'Does one of Mum's men think she's home from Portugal?'

'They're not for your mother, they're for you!' Binkie proclaimed, turning eyes that positively shone with satisfaction onto Tally.

'*Me?*' Tally was satisfyingly thunderstruck by that announcement and she plucked the card from between the older woman's fingertips. Literally tearing off the envelope enclosing the tiny card, she stared down at just two words and a phone number.

Dinner? Sander

'Oh,' she muttered tightly, dropping the card as though it had burned her, while wondering why Sander Volakis handed out such conflicting messages. And did he seriously think that he could just toss her some flowers and she would phone him like an obedient little girl grateful for his attention and eager to forget how he had offended her?

Only five days earlier, Sander had made it painfully clear that he wanted nothing more to do with her and his insinuation that she had slept with him because he was rich had deeply insulted her. Yet he had offered her a dinner date a mere hour later when he dropped her at the train she had caught back to London. She had made it plain that she wasn't interested, so why was he now sending her flowers? An extravagant bunch of very expensive and truly lovely roses, as well.

Binkie wanted to know everything about the sender of the flowers and Tally had to belatedly admit to meeting Sander at Westgrave Manor and share what she knew about him. Reluctant to upset Binkie, she did not tell the disheartening tale of Cosima's antics during that weekend. Her colour fluctuating wildly beneath the older woman's speculative scrutiny, Tally leant heavily on Sander's allegedly bad reputation with women as she spoke. The heady glow of romantic hope in Binkie's eyes slowly began to recede.

While Tally enjoyed arranging the roses and setting the vase in her bedroom she had no intention of making use of Sander Volakis' mobile phone number. In a weak moment she did a search on his name on the Internet and was immediately rewarded with even more good reasons to keep him at a distance. Sander evidently specialised in leggy, famous blondes of the model, entertainment industry celebrity or socialite brand. He dated ladies who wore very small dresses or bikinis and who were papped leaving nightclubs and posing on yachts. And she was quick to remind herself that she hadn't liked him, indeed, had wanted very badly to slap him that morning at Westgrave and had only resisted the urge in a futile effort to reclaim her lost dignity.

Bearing those important facts in mind, Tally accepted that it was very perverse of her to lie awake every night thinking about the volatile Greek and the lean hard-boned lineaments of that unforgettable face of his. Her intelligence put Sander squarely in the incompatible category, but something infinitely less rational and more contrary kept him alive and vibrant in her thoughts. Yet he had put her off sex, she conceded in rueful mortification. All very exciting up to a point and then a rather painful disappointment, she recalled with a grimace, wondering if it would have got better had he continued and then scolding herself for her lingering curiosity. She had learnt a good lesson, she told herself instead. Getting intimate with a stranger was a very bad idea. Sander had assumed that she had sacrificed her virginity in an effort to impress him in some way. So why hadn't he got the message when she refused to see him again?

Cosima phoned her that same morning and confided that Sander had called her to ask for Tally's address. 'Are you seeing him?'

'No, but he sent me flowers,' Tally admitted to satisfy the younger woman's curiosity.

'Dad was very impressed when I told him—'

'You shouldn't have mentioned it,' Tally cut in. 'Nothing's going to happen.'

'Maybe Sander did it for a bet or something,' her sibling suggested. 'Why else would he be chasing you?'

'I don't know, but you seem to have more ideas on that score than I do,' Tally said drily.

Crystal returned that evening from a month-long stay at her current boyfriend's Portuguese villa. Deeply tanned and wearing a lot of gold jewellery, Crystal watched her daughter work on her latest interior design project for college at the dining room table and sighed. 'Don't you ever get tired of being so sensible, Tally?'

'Meaning?' Tally prompted, wondering what had etched shadows like bruises below her mother's fine eyes.

'Peter has decided that he wants a break from me,' she revealed with a shrug that was clearly intended to be careless but which didn't quite pull off the feat. 'Thinks we're getting too serious. Well, we have been practically living together for the past six months…'

Tally picked up on the brittle shaken note in her mother's admission and scrambled out of her seat to wrap her arms round the thin, attractive blonde. Crystal might have a messy love life and be foolish with money, but Tally loved her mother and hated to see her hurting. 'Oh, Mum, I'm sorry!'

'I've been dumped,' Crystal confided thickly, tears glazing her eyes. 'I'm the one who usually does the dumping but I didn't see it coming. I was a fool, I thought Peter was with me for the long haul…'

Tally gave the taller woman a comforting hug. 'Never mind. You'll meet someone else.'

'It's not that easy any more.' Crystal sighed. 'I'm forty-three next birthday, not twenty-three. Men my age want much younger women, and they get them too.'

Navel-gazing wasn't Crystal's thing, however, and within a couple of days Tally's mother had regained her spirits and her extensive net of contacts and busy social calendar played their part in that revival. That weekend, Crystal headed off with a female friend to spend a week in a swanky Scottish castle. Tally, who tried to keep her mother's financial affairs in order, stayed home to be dismayed by the size of the older woman's credit-card bills when they arrived in the post. Crystal could spend as if there were no tomorrow and Peter, a wealthy retiree, was no longer around to support her taste for the high life. Tally resolved to make yet another attempt to persuade her mother to live more within her means. At the start of the following week, she saw Binkie off on her annual summer trip home to Poland where she stayed with her relatives.

The following evening the bell buzzed at seven. Local children had been playing the annoying game of ringing the bell and running away and Tally answered the door with a frown because she expected to find the doorstep empty. But when she found Sander Volakis there instead, his tall, beautifully built body elegantly attired in a charcoal-grey suit teamed with a gold silk tie, she was totally thrown off balance.

One part of her wanted to slam the door and double-lock it, but it was an urge mainly fostered by the awareness that she hadn't combed her hair since lunchtime and was wearing very little make-up. As a young woman who prided herself on her common sense, she was dismayed by her sudden attack of vanity, while the other, more dominant part of her response to his appearance was to simply stare at him and enjoy the view. And when Sander, his jaw line roughened by a five o'clock shadow of stubble that only enhanced his classic masculine features and wide sensual mouth, settled his stunning night-dark eyes on her, he was very much a sight to be savoured.

'Tally,' he purred like a jungle cat on the prowl, studying her from beneath heavy black lashes and very much liking what he saw.

Tally didn't *do* fussy fashion and her denim miniskirt and white cotton top could not have been plainer. Yet rarely had Sander been so aware of a woman's lush curves at breast and hip or her shapely legs. As self-conscious colour stained her creamy cheeks and her green eyes widened and then veiled to conceal their expression an unfamiliar stab of possessiveness gripped him.

'Ask me in,' he urged.

'No,' Tally mumbled, her hand clinging to the door and pushing it a little more closed in rebellion.

'Are you that scared of what might happen?' Sander quipped with a husky sound of amusement.

'Nothing would happen,' Tally fielded stiffly. 'Been there, done that.'

'But you haven't. We've barely begun,' Sander countered forcefully, frustrated by her blank refusal to accept that reality.

'Your choice, then,' Tally traded, her face warm as she made that blunt reminder of the manner in which he had withdrawn from their short-lived intimacy. 'My choice now is not to take it any further.'

'But you're making the *wrong* choice,' Sander told her with impregnable confidence.

'You only think that because it's not what you want and I'm pretty sure that you only ever do what *you* want,' Tally rattled off at equal speed.

'Women don't usually argue with me.'

'Well, you definitely don't want to be spending time with me, Sander,' Tally declared. 'I think I'd always be arguing with you.'

That quip provoked a spontaneous laugh from

Sander that lightened the intensity on his lean, dark, brooding features. 'You challenge me—'

'Which you would enjoy for what...all of five minutes?' Tally cut in unimpressed. 'You know what your problem is? You're bored. That's the only reason you're wasting your time sending me flowers and turning up where you're not welcome.'

For a split second, Sander was stunned by the realisation that she was spot on with that assessment. Of late, the women he took to bed had become very predictable and unexciting. In fact, he could not recall when a woman had last stirred this amount of interest in him and he wondered if it was possible that Tally's resistance was the greatest part of her attraction. Just for once, a woman was not falling into his arms like an overripe plum or making a huge effort to please and flatter him. Indeed Tally Spencer didn't think much of him and had no reservations about letting him know the fact.

'I spoke too frankly and offended you. Is that all you've got against me?'

'No, it's not. You're rich and spoilt and you

think you deserve special treatment. We've got nothing in common, Sander.'

'Except *this*, which you can't deny...' And before Tally could even guess his own intention, he had stepped forward to lower his handsome dark head and seal his mouth to hers in a kiss that hurtled through her unprepared body like a depth charge primed to explode on contact. Shivering, her lips swollen and tingling from the drugging pressure of his, Tally experienced a tugging ache at the very heart of her that left her literally weak at the knees.

Sander slowly lifted his head again, his brilliant gaze glittering gold enticement. 'Dinner tomorrow night. I'll pick you up at eight.'

And with that intense assurance that was so integral a part of him, Sander strode off without awaiting her response. Tally blinked, leant back against the door to dizzily close it and knew that he had played a blinder. That one scorching kiss, which her heart was still racing from, had nothing to do with intellect and had contrived to kill all rational thought within seconds. She thought of not being there when he called to collect her but that struck her as cowardice. Later, she fell into bed in a daze, her brain at war with an overriding but indefensible desire to see him again...

CHAPTER FIVE

TALLY went out to dinner sporting her best jeans teamed with a red top that had a low back.

She refused to agonise over the inadequacies of her under-resourced wardrobe or to get into debt buying a new outfit that she couldn't afford. Nothing could more keenly illustrate the differences between them than her lack of fancy designer togs, but she was not going to feel embarrassed about it, she told herself firmly. She was less proud of the fact that she rifled through her mother's make-up drawer to bolster her own meagre collection of cosmetics and had used eyeliner for only the second time in her life.

'What did you do today?' Sander enquired lazily, his attention dwelling with pleasure on the natural sway of her pouting breasts below the thin fabric of her top as she sat down. The conviction that she wasn't wearing anything beneath it sparked a fire of anticipation in his loins. Thoughts of Tally had interfered with his concentration throughout his working day, an unusual enough development for a male used to keeping his sex life safely corralled within his leisure time. But lust had its own impetus and he recognised the fact, convinced that once his desire was satisfied he would recapture his inherent detachment.

'Work experience with a design firm at Putney,' she revealed, choosing not to add that so far she had been kept well away from the clients and firmly in the background running messages and sourcing supplies. She was eager for the chance to utilise her creative talents. 'I have my final exams in a couple of months, so I'm starting to apply for jobs as well.'

'You're studying?' Sander frowned in surprise. 'Where does your job with Cosima Karydas fit in?'

Tally almost winced at that understandable question and reckoned that she would never make a good liar because her sibling's fibs about their exact relationship had already slipped her mind. 'Oh, that was just a temporary sort of one-off thing,' she muttered uncomfortably. 'I'm actually studying interior design at college and this is my last year.'

'I didn't realise that you were a student.'

'So, tell me about what you do,' Tally urged, keen to change the subject.

Sander mentioned interests in property, pharmaceuticals and the hospitality business and confessed that he was always on the lookout for new investment possibilities. While she could only be impressed by the long hours he evidently worked and his ambition, she sensed that he was never satisfied with his achievements and wondered why not.

Accompanying him into an exquisitely renovated Georgian building with a handsome entrance foyer, she comfortably envisaged the exclusive restaurant she assumed they were heading to next, only to find herself lodged in a lift instead. 'Where's the restaurant?' she prompted.

'There isn't one.' Sander stood back for her to precede him out of the lift and then stuck a key in the lock of the door on the other side of the gracious landing. 'We're eating in...'

Discomfiture immediately gripped Tally, for she had not bargained on a private meal in the intimate setting of his home and would have preferred dining in a public place. Curiosity, however, about his chosen surroundings took her in silence through the first minutes of entering his apartment. The high-tech finish, wooden floors and understated furniture were very masculine but made the most of the classic proportions of the rooms. A dining table was already set with flickering candles in readiness for their meal and her soft pink mouth compressed.

'I would've preferred to have dined out,' she told him candidly.

Surprise at that comment made Sander elevate an ebony brow. 'Why?'

Tally wrinkled her nose and wondered if she dared to be honest a split second before she defied the urge to play dumb for his benefit. 'This feels like a set-up...'

'What the hell does that mean?' Sander frowned as a woman in an apron appeared with a pair of plates and hovered uncertainly. He addressed her in Greek, telling her to go ahead and serve the meal.

Stiff with awkwardness, Tally took a reluctant seat and unfurled her napkin.

'Explain what you meant,' Sander prompted drily.

The starter looked very enticing but the tension in the atmosphere had loosed a flock of uneasy butterflies in the pit of Tally's stomach. She lifted her knife and fork with an appetite that was already on the wane. 'You staged the meal here because you expect me to sleep with you tonight,' she framed curtly and she glanced up, eyes as fresh a green as clover leaves after rain and sparkling with condemnation. 'You've got a hell of a nerve!'

Sander had indeed expected exactly that scenario to develop and had chosen the most convenient backdrop for that desired conclusion to the evening. 'Because I want you? Am I supposed to apologise for that?'

'No, but…' Tally hesitated and then pressed on to speak her mind. 'But I'm more than just a body. I'm a person and I don't want to be here with you if all you're interested in is sex!'

His dark golden gaze veiled, Sander could not restrain an instinctive need to wince at her lack of tact and sophistication. He wondered what possible response she was hoping to receive at such an early stage of their acquaintance. 'I'd like you to stay the night,' he traded without an ounce of embarrassment. 'That's a natural, normal aspiration for me to have.'

Colour ran up below Tally's creamy skin in a flying banner of embarrassment. She had boxed herself into a corner with her declaration, made it clear that while *he* might want only her body, *she* was in the market for something deeper and more meaningful, but that had not been her intention. 'I just don't like the way you make assumptions,' she breathed in a taut undertone.

'You have the right to say no.' Sander voiced that reminder in a tone as smooth as silk.

'Don't patronise me!' Tally fired back at him, throwing down her knife and fork and pushing her plate away in an angry gesture.

'You're very quick-tempered,' Sander remarked.

Discomfiture attacking her in receipt of that opinion, Tally tugged her plate back and began doggedly to eat, barely tasting the delicious dish in her determination to appear calm and composed.

'Always ready and willing to have a fight with me,' Sander continued.

'I don't even know what I'm doing here with you!' Tally exclaimed helplessly.

'Oh, that's easy,' Sander quipped, filling her wine glass. 'You're with me for the exact same reason I'm with you. You can't stay away.'

The truth of that statement hit Tally as hard as a head-on collision. She looked at him and it was as if he had cast a spell on her, for it was a challenge even to *look* away, never mind walk away. Desire had dug greedy claws into her body, awakening the hormones that inspired craving and stealing her freedom of choice. He infuriated her and he had insulted her, yet she had still agreed to dinner. Suddenly even madder with herself than she was with him, Tally pushed back her chair and stood up. 'I shouldn't be here. Don't worry, I'll make my own way home.'

Sander slowly rose upright, keen dark golden eyes locked to her hectically flushed face. 'Are you always as impetuous as this?'

Tally paled, wondering if she shared more with her mother than she had ever appreciated because he seemed to draw out a side of her nature that she was unfamiliar with: an ardent, capricious, insecure side, which made her feel incredibly vulnerable. Suddenly she was acting a world away from the stable, sensible and fairly unemotional young woman she had always assumed that she was. He made her want things she had never wanted, like long straight blonde hair, a body the shape of a pencil and endless legs. He made her want to be irresistible, the sort of woman men fought over and loved to the brink of insanity.

'You make me impulsive,' she admitted grudgingly.

'You have a weird effect on me too,' Sander confided with an eloquent shift of two lean brown hands. 'I was convinced that I wanted nothing more to do with you, but the minute I saw you leaving Westgrave Manor I drove after you and asked you out to dinner.'

And Tally's barrier of apprehension and insecurity tumbled down there and then because those revealing, almost bemused words of his soothed her concern and eased her distrust. It didn't sound like a male pickup line and she had heard most of them from the smarmy, 'Did it hurt when you fell out of heaven?' to the coarse, 'Fancy a shag?' It sounded as though he was telling the truth and that he was equally mystified by the way he reacted to her.

Once again she sat down and the main course was served. Finally starting to relax, she ate and asked questions about the flat, for the strikingly effective combination of contemporary décor married to Georgian classic elegance appealed to her creative instincts. Sander told her that he had renovated the entire building before converting it into apartments, keeping the most spacious for his own use. She chattered about her college course and let down her guard to the extent that she had to swallow back an unwise reference to her father, before confiding that one day she wanted to open her own design company.

In the lounge Sander sat back and enjoyed her bubbling animation. He found her surprisingly good company; she had none of the conceit and superficiality he was accustomed to meeting with in women. Tally met his stunning dark golden eyes and felt the intensity there to the extent that her mouth ran dry and her heartbeat accelerated. He reached out a graceful hand and removed her wine glass from her grasp to set it aside. And, without the smallest hesitation, she shifted closer, wanting, needing to connect. Long fingers curving to her slim shoulder, he bent his head to toy with her soft full lips until the heat of anticipation was tingling and burning between her thighs. What shocked her was how very quickly and powerfully she felt the pull of his sexual magnetism.

He kissed her softly and then he kissed her hard, his lips urgent and demanding around the skilled plunge of his tongue into the sensitive interior of her mouth. She clung to him as if he were the only rock in a storm and gasped in startled response when he burrowed below her top to close a hungry hand over the fullness of her breasts. As he massaged the pouting swells and the tender prominence of her nipples with skilled fingers excitement began to hurtle through her in an unstoppable wave.

'Let's move this to the bedroom,' Sander urged thickly, hauling her upright and pausing to kiss her with a passionate dominance that lit up every skin cell in her quivering body.

The yearning hit a high and she wound her arms round him and kissed him back with the same passion, loving the taste of his strong sensual mouth and the scent of his skin. With a gruff sound of satisfaction he lifted her up into his arms and strode into the bedroom across the landing.

He settled her down on the bed and suddenly tensed. 'Something I forgot to say,' he breathed, beautiful eyes welded to her flushed face. 'I don't do exclusivity…'

'Okay,' Tally fielded without even having to think about it. 'You don't do exclusivity. I don't do sex.'

Sander froze and slowly dragged his hands from her. 'You can't be serious.'

Bright green eyes focused on him. 'Do other women settle for that, "I don't do exclusivity" malarkey?'

'With all the options out there, who wants to be tied down? They settle for it,' Sander asserted.

Tally sighed and shook her head. 'I *won't*,' she said almost apologetically, her gaze clinging ruefully to his lean, darkly handsome features.

Sander groaned out loud and fell back a step. She could not have missed the pronounced bulge of his erection below his jeans. 'You have me over a...barrel...'

'Or, in this case...a bed?' Tally suggested, struggling to cool the tingling heat at the centre of her body with will power alone but stubbornly unprepared to compromise. 'It's your choice.'

'This is ridiculous.' Seething frustration filled Sander when she fired back the same reminder he had used with her only minutes earlier. 'It's not as though you're still a virgin, either.'

'I am not sharing a bed with you while you continue to sleep with other women.' Tally planted each word like a solid foot settling into newly poured concrete and then she slid her own feet off the bedspread he had placed her on and began to search for her discarded shoes.

'That's like blackmail,' Sander launched at her grittily, something akin to sheer disbelief momentarily clouding his stunning dark eyes as he stared at her. 'You are so bloody demanding!'

'You're a good teacher.' Tally almost laughed at his expression, but she had no softness in her on the score of fidelity and it would be a long time before she forgot the ruthless expertise of his seduction of her at Westgrave. Then she had got so carried away that she hadn't known what she was doing, but this time around she was trying to look out for herself and spot the pitfalls in advance. And the pitfalls of getting involved with Sander Volakis, she sensed ruefully, could be huge if she wasn't careful.

Sander watched her reach the door and it seemed like a battle of wits between them then because he was constitutionally incapable of surrender. His body rigid with the ache of fierce self-control, his eyes fiery, he watched her gather up her bag and emerge from the lounge to depart.

'I'll call a taxi,' Tally told him breezily.

Later he didn't remember moving, but he must have done because when time mysteriously moved on he had her lush body pinned up against the back of the front door and he was crushing her sultry, satiny, sexy mouth under his and drinking deep of an ardour that perfectly matched his own. It was glorious.

'Sander…' she muttered shakily when he allowed her to breathe again.

'For as long as I want you, there won't be anyone else,' he intoned in a raw undertone. 'But we mightn't last five minutes…'

Encountering those wrathful dark golden eyes Tally recognised how much giving way to her rules had cost him and knew that he was saving face. She suppressed a smile born of understanding rather than triumph. Something about his explosive streak of volatility fired a tender rush of feeling inside her and she stretched up to press her mouth to his again in an unwittingly soothing gesture.

In the bedroom he pulled off his shirt, lean, hard muscle flexing below his bronzed hair-roughened skin. She was kicking off her shoes again when he peeled her out of her top and he had to pull her into his arms to prevent her from unbalancing and tumbling backwards. He lowered her down onto the bed, scorching dark golden eyes raking over the upward swell of her full breasts with unashamed appreciation. As he unsnapped her jeans and tugged them off Tally was almost dizzy on a sense of her own daring. The longing to be closer to him and pulse of need in her pelvis were too strong for her to fight and she was trying to give in with grace and fight, the shyness that made it such a challenge for her to lie there nude but for a small pair of knickers.

Air was forced from her lungs in a gasp when he stroked the creamy mounds already taut with desire and caught a tender throbbing pink peak between his lips to lash the swollen tip with his tongue. Her fluttering hands closed into his cropped black hair, holding him to her, dropping to his wide strong shoulders when he reared up and reclaimed her reddened mouth with erotic urgency. He stripped off his jeans and his boxers in an impatient surge of activity.

The sense of liquid warmth between her thighs increased when she felt the urgent thrust of his manhood against her hip. Her body was gearing up for the next step, chemical reactions taking place to ensure that any halt would be a savage disappointment. The memory of her first painful experience did not dim her anticipation or the wild rise of her hunger when he scored an explorative fingertip over the damp crotch of her knickers. She felt so sensitive there, embarrassingly aware of what had always been a private part of her body. Pulling her close, Sander hooked a hand into the waistband of her last garment and removed it.

'I'll make it wonderful, *glikia mou*,' Sander promised as she lay there momentarily tense, uncertainty alight in her expressive green eyes.

Ready to be convinced and mortified that he could read her so easily, Tally veiled her eyes. His hands glided over her in a light exploration, smoothing her skin, caressing every curve and dimple. His leisurely approach ensured that her apprehension ebbed to be replaced by melting warmth and a ready tingling of awareness in the more erogenous zones. He ran his tongue down the valley between her breasts, paused to toy with her swollen nipples and then moved lower, down over the quivering tightness of her stomach to the delicate pink flesh between her trembling thighs.

'No,' she told him in strong embarrassment, locking her ankles together to deny him access.

Sander slid up level with her troubled gaze again and ran a reassuring finger along the taut line of her lower lip. 'I want to give you the maximum possible pleasure,' he husked. 'I want to rewrite our history.'

'You can't—what happened, happened,' Tally protested tightly as he parted her ankles with a twist of his knee and his foot and sent skilled fingers gliding across her taut inner thigh.

'Trust me.' At the first intimate touch her eyes slid shut and her hands tightened into fists of restraint, for she had an instinctive fear of losing control. He pressed his mouth to the shallow indentation of her navel and her legs eased apart.

There was a waiting greedy hum of arousal at the heart of her, a helpless yearning for the unknown.

With his tongue and his fingers he probed and explored the tender flesh, teaching her about nerve endings that she didn't know she had until they went downright crazy under the onslaught of his expert caresses. As the hot tingle of excitement rose her hips began to squirm into the mattress and then rise in answer to the long fingers pleasuring her tight inner channel. He reached up to tug at her protuberant nipples and the hot gathering tightness in her pelvis just surged unstoppably to a peak and hot splintering pleasure shot through her like lightning. She cried out in shock as the waves of bliss engulfed her, all control wrested from her.

The orgasmic quivers were still travelling through her when Sander hauled her under him and surged with a hungry groan of appreciation into her slick, tight body. In the aftermath of that earth-shattering climax, Tally was still so sensitive that she cried out again—not with pain, but with a pleasure that was almost agonising as Sander flexed his hips and sank into her slow and deep, stretching her to full capacity. Hunger gripped her afresh as he began to move faster. The ripples of pleasure began to build again with the delicious friction and she bucked beneath him in wild excitement. He pushed her legs back to rise higher over her, his lean dark face fevered and urgent. The intensity of sensation sent spasms of delight through her. Her inner contractions made her tighten round him and he groaned in appreciation just seconds before her excitement hit an unbearable peak and flung her headlong back into the red hot mists of pleasure.

Filled with wonderment at what she had just experienced, Tally was shy and she lay still while the sweet waves of ecstasy slowly receded to leave her earthbound again. It shook her that she had been so ignorant of what her own body was capable of and it scared her as well, for she knew that such physical pleasure could only prove addictive.

Sander had never experienced such intense excitement with a woman. She was even more responsive than he had hoped. He held her close, his heart still pounding from his exertions, his lean, powerful length hot and damp and potent with masculinity. He was already getting aroused again. 'You were amazing,' he murmured thickly. 'I knew we would be pure magic together, *glikia mou*.'

'I've got so much to learn,' she muttered in a daze.

'I know and I'm very much looking forward to expanding your experience.' A wicked smile lodged on his wide sensual mouth, Sander closed a hand over a full firm breast, rubbing a still tender pink peak between thumb and forefinger.

'So this isn't a one-night stand,' Tally gathered with a little shiver of hunger, heat rising in the pit of her stomach like a hot pool of melting honey.

'I left those behind when I was a teenager.' Sander turned her round and brought her fingers down to his throbbing erection, luxuriant black lashes screening his eyes in a sensual expression as he silently showed her how to please him.

A new and startling sense of power assailed Tally while she noted how susceptible he was to her touch, but she also discovered that arousing him aroused her equally and, just minutes later, he flipped her over, pulled her back against him and sank into her again. There was no limit, she discovered, to her pleasure, for once again the world disintegrated around her and her body soared to heights she had not even dreamt of. Afterwards she was more tired than she had ever been in her life.

'I think it's time that I took you home,' Sander suggested, throwing back the sheet to stride into the bathroom and switching on the shower.

On the drive back through the quiet streets, he said softly, 'Can I give you a piece of advice without you taking offence?'

'Depends on what the advice is,' Tally told him sleepily.

'Don't get serious about me. We had great sex and I like your company but I'm not looking for a live-in partner, a wife or even a serious girl-friend.'

'Oh, for goodness' sake,' Tally exclaimed, losing colour in receipt of such candour.

'Now that that is said, we won't misunderstand each other,' Sander returned unapologetically.

'It might also be a good idea for you to consider some form of reliable contraception.'

Tally rolled her eyes and sighed. 'That's my business—'

'No, it's our mutual business while we're sharing a bed,' Sander riposted.

'I'm not going to fall pregnant on you,' Tally declared very drily, guessing the source of his concern. Although he had taken precautions when they had made love she had already decided to visit her doctor and take measures on her own behalf.

'I've seen friends dragged through that experience and no matter how they deal with the problem, it always seems to turn nasty,' Sander remarked grimly. 'Don't ever put me through that, Tally.'

Tally startled him by laughing spontaneously. 'Do you always focus on the worst-case scenario?'

Sander rested magnetic dark eyes on her, his expression grave and unamused. 'In that field, yes...'

CHAPTER SIX

'HURRY up,' Sander urged impatiently into his phone. 'I'm double-parked!'

'I'm almost there,' Tally gasped, running out of breath as she charged past the shops and up to the sleek silver Ferrari awaiting her arrival.

Slinging her bag of files in ahead of her, she almost fell into the passenger seat in her haste. All her attention was reserved for the breath-takingly handsome male at the steering wheel. The lean dark beauty of Sander's features always enthralled her. Sander had spent the previous week in Athens and she had missed him intolerably while he'd been away. That was why she was cutting classes to meet up with him in the afternoon, breaking one of her most unbreakable rules on his behalf. Now, as she looked at him with shining green eyes, common sense and cool were the furthest things from her mind.

In his driving mirror, Sander had been watching a traffic warden with a hand-held device in readiness to book him with a parking offence, but when Tally tumbled into the car, dressed in her student apparel of jeans and a brightly coloured tunic, his stunning dark golden eyes welded to her instead. In a movement that lacked his usual measured grace, he lifted a lean hand to close his fingers into her tousled tangle of curls and tip up her face. As usual she was bubbling with chatter, which emerged in confused half-sentences, her overwhelming excitement and delight at seeing him again as unfeigned as a child's. Her warmth and naturalness had as much appeal for Sander, the child of rigidly cool and undemonstrative parents, as the clarity of her eyes, flawless skin and those pink pillowy and oh-so-kissable lips of hers. Without hesitation he bent his head and claimed her tempting mouth in a long drugging kiss that sent naked excitement snaking through her in an insane rush.

Before the traffic warden had finished tapping

in his vehicle registration details, Sander was already driving off. Tally was in a daze, battening down the fierce hunger he had roused so easily even while she longed to drag him back into her arms. A glance down at the trouser fabric moulded to the hard swollen ridge of his manhood informed her that the desire was mutual. She had worried that he might seek sexual solace elsewhere while he was away but the revealing heat of his powerful libido reassured her even while she knew that there were no guarantees.

After all, Tally had set out on their association with the very rational resolve that she would be sensible and not allow herself to get too attached to Sander Volakis. His reputation, his age and the very differences between them in the status and wealth stakes had all warned her not to take too optimistic or long-term a view of their relationship. But regardless of those facts, they had now stayed together for seven weeks and the heat of the attraction between them had yet to show any sign of abating.

Binkie had met Sander very briefly when he'd picked Tally up one evening and had pronounced him 'charming' while Crystal, who was currently staying in Spain with a recently widowed friend, had only had dire warnings to make on the score of her daughter's liaison with a Greek entrepreneur.

'The most you'll ever have with Sander Volakis will be a steamy affair before he gets bored and moves on to some other woman,' Crystal contended with a cynical twist of her lips. 'I'm telling you that for your own good. If you're prepared it will hurt less.'

'I know Sander's not in love with me,' Tally admitted rather tightly, although she continued to keep a valiant smile pinned to her face. 'That doesn't mean I can't be happy while it lasts.'

'As long as you accept that you don't have a future with him.'

'I accepted that at the start,' Tally fielded a tinge drily. 'We're both young and single, so of course it's not going to last for ever.'

Having said all the right, level-headed things, Tally had become conscious that day that she wasn't really fooling anyone, least of all herself. She adored Sander, absolutely adored him. Just the sound of his voice on the phone made her day and a glance from his dark deep-set eyes could tie her in knots and make her burn with longing. Even though she had not intended to fall madly in love with him, it had happened all the same.

She was relieved that Sander had not yet met her mother, for Crystal had never overcome her bitterness at the way her child's father had treated her and Tally did not trust the older woman not to make some scornful and embarrassing comment about her daughter's Greek parentage. Sander still didn't know that Anatole Karydas was Tally's father but she saw no reason why she should tell him, because what difference would it make to him? It was not as though her father took any interest in her life or even bothered to stay in regular contact with her.

Rushing into the lift to keep up with Sander's long impatient stride, Tally was feeling quite dizzy when the lift whirred up to his apartment. As goose bumps rose on her skin and perspiration dampened her short upper lip she also felt slightly sick. It was far from being the first time she had felt under par in recent weeks and once again she resolved to visit her doctor when she could find the time. Having started taking the contraceptive pill to protect herself from pregnancy, she was beginning to suspect that the particular brand she was using might not suit her because she was suffering from increasingly frequent attacks of nausea.

Sander scooped her up in the hall and kissed her hard, the cool he practised in public places banished as his hands roved over her, smoothing up below the tunic to find the ripe curves of her breasts. An earthy groan of appreciation escaped him as he pushed her bra out of his path and kneaded the firm mounds that tumbled into his palms. 'I'm so hot and ready I could take you here...'

'I missed you too,' Tally confided, engaged in wresting him out of his jacket, which fell on the tiled floor.

'*Skase!* Shut up,' he told her, urgently covering her mouth again. 'You're talking too much...'

While he kissed her breathless, stoking the flames of arousal already quivering through her, Sander pulled her through to the bedroom. His eagerness to make love to her thrilled Tally and made up for other omissions. He had yet to introduce her to any friends, other than those they had accidentally run into when out. He had never asked her to stay the whole night with him. He also never invited her out more than forty-eight hours in advance or said anything that might allow her to assume that they would still be together in a few weeks' time.

Having whipped away her tunic and bra and trailed off her jeans in speedy succession, Sander stood by the bed stripping from his suit. He was so aroused he was in pain and had barely slept the night before. He had never had such great sexual rapport with a woman and he loved the fact that Tally had not known any of his friends or indeed his rivals before him. She was exclusively his in a way no other woman had ever contrived to be and very much his creation between the sheets. He was convinced that that was why he enjoyed being with her so much and why he had yet to become bored with her.

Watching her lover undress, Tally came up on her knees. She took the level of his arousal as a compliment. There was a hum of answering desire low in her pelvis, a tingling, dampening swelling between her thighs. She bent her head to caress his hard shaft with her tongue and her lips and a raw sound of pleasure escaped him before he sank his fingers into her hair and pulled back from her. 'I want to come inside you,' he breathed thickly. 'And I'm way too revved up already, *latria mou.*'

Sander having reassured her with a recent health check, and taking account of the fact that she had started taking the contraceptive pill, Tally had agreed to his making love to her without using a condom. She knew that her trust in him was mirrored by his in her, because he had admitted that he had never trusted a woman sufficiently before to dispense with that added safety barrier.

He eased her down on the bed beside him and closed his mouth to a swollen pink nipple to draw it deeply between his lips while his fingers stroked the tender tissue between her thighs to establish her readiness. A whimper of appreciative sound was dragged from her as he rubbed her tiny bud of pleasure. Her hips rose and then squirmed and her back arched while he probed her with an exploring finger. With a hungry groan he sheathed himself in her honeyed heat, stretching the delicate walls of her body with his thick hardness. She cried out, eager for every sensation, clutching at him with frantic hands as a starburst of powerful excitement engulfed her and he began to pound into her tight channel with strong sensual need.

So intense was Tally's excitement that she writhed under him as the paroxysms of pleasure washed through her in pulsing waves that were hitting closer and closer together. Their passion drove them both to an explosive conclusion. The tension provoked by that almost agonising excitement peaked at an incredible climax that saw Tally buck and cry out as his magnificent body shuddered over hers. In the same glorious instant of release he spilled his life force into her with an uninhibited shout of satisfaction.

After a moment of recovery, Sander settled smouldering dark eyes welded with concern to her hectically flushed face. 'I got carried away—did I hurt you?'

'No, of course not,' Tally declared breathlessly, her eyes shining and her body heavy with an overload of voluptuous pleasure as she wrapped both arms round him in an unashamedly enthusiastic hug.

'I never quite forget the first time, *latria mou*.' Raking long brown fingers through his tousled black hair, Sander tolerated being hugged and even enjoyed her affection in a way he chose not to focus on or examine in any greater depth. She was a touchy-feely girl, designed to melt when it came to animals, kids and sob stories, and that was part and parcel of what he viewed as her soft, naturally feminine nature.

'What did you do in Athens?' Tally questioned, lacing her fingers through his in an insistent gesture.

'I don't want to talk… I want to go to sleep,' Sander teased.

'You *can't*—you've been away a week!' Tally complained feelingly. 'So, Athens?'

'My father wants me to move home and get

involved in his company and my mother wants me to marry a nice Greek girl, four of whom she lined up for a big dinner party they staged while I was there...'

None of that information was welcome to Tally but she kept on lightly smiling for she was conscious that she had asked and should be grateful that he had answered honestly. 'Fancy any of them?'

'No, don't fancy getting married either,' Sander confided, cupping a hand to a plump breast and massaging the pink pouting peak to stiffened sensitivity, smiling as her spine began to arch in response and a little breathy sound escaped her parted lips. 'Why would I want anyone else when I have you in my bed? Do you know, I think your beautiful breasts are getting bigger?'

Tally went pink. 'I think it's the pills I'm taking.'

Sander gave her an all-male grin that had a wicked edge of pure sensuality. 'I'm not complaining. I love your body. By the way, we're going out tonight.'

'Where?'

'A friend is having a private party at a club,' Sander proffered, springing upright and bending down to scoop her off the mattress. 'Time for a shower, lazybones.'

Tally was thrilled that she was finally about to meet some of his friends. 'I'll need to go home to get changed—'

'No, you won't,' Sander asserted. 'I've taken care of that.'

'What are you talking about?'

'You'll see…' Tugging her under the water with him, Sander slicked her with shower gel and concentrated heavily on her breasts. Her nipples had become impossibly sensitive and, in tune with her gasps, it wasn't long before it became obvious that washing was the last thing on Sander's mind as well.

'Want me?' he breathed, grazing the swollen buds of her breasts with knowing fingers.

'*So much,*' she ground out between clenched teeth of restraint, shaking with the desire he had reawakened.

Angling his hips out from the wall, he lifted her and brought her down on his throbbing erection before flipping round to brace her against the tiles. What followed was energetic, earthy and incredibly exciting and, in the aftermath, she was so exhausted she lay up against him in a tangle of splayed limbs, struggling to catch her breath.

Wrapped in a towel in the bedroom, she finally discovered why he had said that there would be no need for her to go home and change. He strode out to the hall and reappeared with a pile of boxes, which he dumped in a casual heap on the bed.

'New clothes,' he told her cheerfully.

Tally froze, disconcerted. 'You've bought me clothes?'

'If I have to take you out one more time in that black dress, or that one with the flashy jewelled neckline, I'll rip them in two!' Sander complained. 'You need a new outfit and here it is.'

He tugged open the first box and tipped the contents out, so that a spill of expensive emerald-green fabric slithered out onto the bed. It only took a glimpse of the famous designer label for her to recoil. 'That dress must have cost hundreds...I can't accept it from you!'

It was the first time that Tally had ever really irritated Sander and he had to bite back a derisive response. He knew how much appearances counted with his friends and while he appreciated the fact that, unlike most of her predecessors, she didn't expect him to continually lavish expensive gifts on her, he thought she took independence too far for comfort.

In silent determination he broke open the other boxes and tumbled their contents out onto the bed. Tally flushed as she noticed the cobweb-fine underwear, and stockings and shoes that accompanied the dress. Her chin came up at a defiant angle. 'Has my lack of a designer wardrobe caused you embarrassment?'

'No, but I know enough about women to know that you will be embarrassed if you don't wear this tonight,' he completed smoothly.

Mortified by his candour, Tally looked away from him and wished that money weren't such an embarrassing subject. This was the first time it had caused trouble between them. His annoyance did not pass her by, for although he had said nothing she knew him well enough to read the tension etched in his lean dark features and the coolness in his gaze. Her pride warred with her reluctance to stage a major argument over a gift that many women would have gratefully, even joyously accepted from him. For the first time she wondered if her lack of a presentable wardrobe had dissuaded him from taking her out to mix in his usual circles.

'I'm even more embarrassed by you doing this,' Tally confided in a rush. 'But I can see that you intended to be kind and generous and even thoughtful, and I don't want to be ungrateful. But please don't ever buy me clothes again.'

'I don't want you to look out of place or feel uncomfortable with my friends,' Sander admitted.

She almost told him that if that was the case he had the wrong friends but bit back the comment as the atmosphere was still tense and he was volatile.

She let her fingers glide over the costly material of the dress. 'It's a gorgeous colour,' she conceded stiffly, offering an olive branch.

'The instant I saw it, I knew you would look amazing in it,' Sander confided, hauling her into his arms and staring down at her with flattering intensity.

And there and then she forgave him absolutely, even though her brain was still telling her that it was wrong to let him buy her expensive clothes. 'Will you be annoyed if it doesn't fit?'

'This isn't the first time I've bought a dress for a woman,' Sander imparted drily.

'Too much information,' Tally muttered, vanishing back into the bathroom to tame and dry her wet hair.

'I bought you emerald and diamond earrings as well.' As Tally froze at the vanity mirror and spun round Sander dealt her a might-as-well-be-hung-for-a-sheep-as-a-lamb look of challenge.

Tally parted bloodless lips. 'I don't want them.'

In the doorway, Sander flung his arms wide in a gesture that expressed his frustration. 'What is your problem? You give me a great deal of pleasure. Why is it wrong for me to show you my appreciation in the only way open to me?'

Put like that, it made her sound small-minded

and ungrateful and she went pink. 'Accepting costly gifts from you just doesn't feel right,' she framed.

'Don't be difficult,' Sander censured. 'You should never question generosity.'

She thought about the Greek girls his mother had lined up in Athens and chewed at her lower lip rather than toss a provocative retort. But if she wasn't careful, she thought ruefully, loving Sander would make a coward of her and she would become so focused on keeping him happy that she would lose herself. It was a scary consideration and while she dried her hair and renewed her make-up she swore to herself that even love wouldn't make a doormat of her, wouldn't make her do and say and accept things she didn't believe in.

Infuriatingly, for she would have loved to criticise, the dress was elegantly restrained in shape and length and it fitted as though it had been specially made for her. He handed her a jewel box and she extracted earrings fashioned as glittering stars with an emerald jewel at the centre.

'They reminded me of your eyes...'

Knowing how starry-eyed she was around him, Tally laughed and put them on. The earrings were gorgeous, catching and reflecting the light like miniature chandeliers. Indeed the combined effect of the jewellery and the dress was impressive, she acknowledged grudgingly, wanting and needing him to be proud of her even if that meant swallowing her own pride and independence.

Sander took her to a swanky London nightclub, well known for attracting celebrities and the rich. On the way to their table, he was hailed from all sides with waves and calls and it was obvious he was a regular. He ordered champagne but Tally's tummy was slightly dodgy again and she stuck to mineral water, rather than run the risk of worsening the nausea. Sander stood up to talk to friends and briefly introduced her to young women who were barely willing to acknowledge Tally's existence at his side. She saw a girl push something into his pocket and when they were briefly alone insisted on knowing what it was.

Sander drew out a card bearing a phone number and a personal message and crushed it between his fingers before she could contrive to read what had been written. 'It happens all the time,' he said dismissively as Tally stared at the card in shock at such bold behaviour. 'Some of these women would kill to land a rich man. I ignore such invitations.'

Tally was disturbed by the number of come-ons he received even with her actually sitting beside him. Girls in opulent micro-minis that revealed a great deal more than they concealed approached him throughout the evening and eventually, to get peace from the constant interruptions, Sander took Tally to another table in the VIP area, which was guarded by burly bouncers. There, ironically, however, he met up with the only female who actually bothered Tally. He brought a slender exquisite Greek girl back from the bar where she had been standing with companions.

'Oleia Telis, an old friend of mine...Tally Spencer...'

Oleia, who was so petite in build she made Tally feel like an elephant, managed to keep on smiling brightly while withering Tally with a glacial look of hostility. The brunette talked exclusively to Sander in Greek and clearly amused him because he laughed quite a lot. Against the backdrop of the music Tally could not hear their conversation, and within minutes Oleia had slid her tiny figure between Sander and Tally and had spread a possessive hand on his lean muscular thigh. When the flirtatious brunette dragged him off to dance, Tally headed for the cloakroom where she was stunned to turn away from the washbasins and find herself being confronted by three young women whom she recognised as Oleia's friends from the VIP area.

'Why don't you go home?' one of them demanded with a venomous appraisal. 'Sander's dancing with Oleia. They don't need you hanging around them like a bad smell.'

'Sander brought me here with him tonight,' Tally responded, lifting her head high, determined not to be intimidated by their approach.

'He's known Oleia all his life. He's slumming with you. Why can't you take the hint and back off?' another of the girls asked maliciously.

Her cheeks burning, Tally pushed past the unpleasant trio and returned to the VIP area, hovering at the edge of the dance floor only to see Oleia plastered up against Sander like a second skin with her arms linked tightly round his neck. Tally watched as the tiny beautiful brunette stretched up to kiss Sander and shamelessly rotated her pelvis against his. She watched and while she watched Sander didn't push Oleia away. Her heart sinking down to her toes and her sensitive tummy churning, Tally turned hurriedly away from that distressing spectacle and pulled out her mobile phone to text Sander.

'I won't stand for you kissing another woman. We're finished. I'm going home.'

A bouncer hailed a cab for her and she climbed in, caught up in a daze of sick disbelief, even while she took her time in the dim hope that he might immediately read the message and follow her. How *could* it be over just like that? Without any warning? Without him first demonstrating some evidence of his loss of interest in her? Of course possibly the fairy-like brunette had simply proved more temptation than Sander could withstand. Shell-shocked, Tally set her phone beside her bed and lay there wide awake waiting for Sander to respond to her text. But there was no reply, either then or by the following morning, when she wakened at dawn and succumbed to the realisation that Sander's continuing silence confirmed that their relationship was over.

Her misery was evidently too much for her tender stomach. She endured her worst attack of nausea to date and then rushed into the bathroom where she was ingloriously sick. Her breasts were uncomfortably tender as well. Indeed everything felt wrong in her world. No matter what way she looked at what had happened she could not forgive Sander or excuse his behaviour with Oleia Telis. Still suffering from a sick headache, she went to class and made an appointment to see a doctor that afternoon because she reckoned it was past time that she had her digestive troubles checked out.

The appointment was brief. Once she had outlined her concerns, the doctor began to discuss alternative forms of contraception but, since her relationship with Sander was over, Tally saw no reason to continue the course of pills and said she would simply stop taking them. The doctor suggested that she have a blood test, which a nurse conducted, and then Tally returned to college. When she got home, Binkie told her that the medical practice had phoned to arrange a second appointment for her with the doctor the next day. Binkie also passed on the news that Tally's mother was flying back from Spain later that evening.

Tally opened her eyes the following morning in a downbeat mood. Sander's total silence was downright insulting, she decided angrily, refusing to acknowledge the painful sense of loss and disillusionment she was suppressing. The way Sander was treating her she might as well have been a one-night stand! Evidently she had never meant anything much to him and the bonds she had believed they were developing had existed more in her imagination than in reality. It was a lesson to her for falling in love with so little encouragement to do so!

Just the knowledge that she could no longer even text Sander gave Tally a hollow feeling inside. It was over, it was *really* over, she reflected painfully while she waited to see her doctor. The older man greeted her with a rather taut smile and she sat down rather anxiously.

'I had the practice manager make this appointment because the blood test you had done yesterday revealed that you're pregnant,' the doctor explained.

Tally paled. 'But that's not possible...I mean, I was taking contraceptive pills—'

'It's a low-dose pill though. Were you careful to take other precautions during the first three weeks?' the older man asked. 'Did you miss taking any pills? Or were you sick at any stage? I notice you were taking antibiotics for an infection during the second week. Any of those things could have interfered with the effectiveness of your birth control.'

Tally opened her mouth and then closed it again just as quickly. She *had* missed taking one pill altogether and she was fairly sure that Sander had stopped using condoms before the end of the third week. As for the added risk of taking antibiotics, at the same time she had had no idea that the medication could interfere with her contraception. Reeling with shock, she submitted to an examination before asking in a small voice how pregnant she was.

'I estimate about six weeks.'

Much of his advice about taking more rest and eating a healthy diet went over Tally's head because she couldn't think straight. She was having Sander's baby and they had already broken up. The guy didn't even care enough to have contacted her in the past forty-eight hours! She might have walked away but he had let her go. In desperate need of someone to talk to about her dilemma Tally skipped her afternoon class and went home to confide in Binkie.

The older woman could not conceal her dismay and concern. 'Oh, Tally,' she sighed unhappily. 'What will you do?'

Tally closed her hands together. 'I'm going to have the baby. Mum had me in similar circumstances,' she pointed out.

'Your parents were engaged and your mother still hoped that there would be a marriage.'

'Sander and I aren't together anymore,' Tally admitted reluctantly.

'But you'll have to tell him about the baby…'

'What are you two whispering about?' a third voice interposed from the kitchen doorway. 'What baby?'

Tally glanced up in lively dismay to see her mother standing there clad in a floaty black negligee and matching nightdress.

'Tally's pregnant,' Binkie explained very quietly as she rose from the table. 'I'll leave you to talk.'

'Pregnant!' Crystal exclaimed furiously. 'By Sander Volakis?'

Tally nodded. 'I haven't told him yet.'

Crystal winced. 'Oh, darling, you're so naïve. You won't see him for dust when you do tell him.'

Tally jerked a stiff shoulder. 'It's his baby too and he should know. Unfortunately we've broken up.'

'Just wait until your father hears about this!' Crystal almost seemed to savour the idea of telling the older man about his daughter's condition, her green eyes gleaming with a touch of malice.

Tally frowned. 'Why on earth would you tell my father?' she demanded in embarrassment. 'I don't want him told. It's none of his business.'

When she thought about it, Tally felt no concern about Crystal sharing the news of her conception. As far as Tally was aware, Anatole's hostility towards Crystal, the mother of his illegitimate daughter, had not abated one whit over the years and her parents very rarely spoke to each other.

'You're too young to be landed with a baby.' Crystal sighed. 'You should consider a termination.'

'I'll consider all my options,' Tally muttered purely for the sake of peace. She went up to her room and texted Sander to tell him that she needed to see him urgently. There was no diplomatic way of breaking such news and the sooner it was done, the better, she thought unhappily. He would be anything but pleased; she knew that already thanks to his candour at the outset of their affair. But deep down inside, she nourished a little kernel of hope that his reaction to her announcement would be more generous than he had given her reason to expect...

CHAPTER SEVEN

His lean, darkly handsome features brooding, the banked fire of his anger illuminating his dark eyes to smouldering gold, Sander released his breath in a slow hiss when his PA indicated that Tally had arrived. He was glad he had told her to come and see him at his office. The businesslike surroundings would keep the meeting brief and to the point. After all, what was there left to say? Her walkout at the club had outraged him. He had brought friends into the VIP area to meet her, only to find that she had departed, and her peremptory text that delivered judgement without a hearing had only exacerbated his mood.

Tally had put on leggings, pumps and a long line T-shirt in a berry colour to face Sander. She wanted to look normal, not as though she had made a special effort, and yet she had spent over an hour on her hair and her make-up and had changed clothes three times over, before finally looking in the mirror and conceding that absolutely no power on earth was ever going to give her teeny tiny Oleia's cute doll-like proportions or her flawlessly pretty face. She knew she was jealous and that made her feel mean-spirited.

Stepping inside the spacious office, she focused on Sander. He was as gorgeous as a spectacular sunset, she reflected dizzily, all sleek dark Mediterranean good looks and height and muscular power drenched with buckets of pure sex appeal. He was lounging back against the edge of his desk in an attitude of relaxation, no doubt staged to look super-cool and controlled. That masculine stance and stubborn, insolent attitude were *so* Sander that Tally could have screamed with vexation. She was not so easily fooled as she could read the tension in his broad shoulders and the angles of his high cheekbones, not to mention the compression of his lower lip. And his pretence of cool simply gave her a horrendous desire to slap him and tell him to give her a real human reaction. But, no doubt, she would soon receive exactly that from him when she told him about the baby. *Their* baby, she adjusted thoughtfully, and she felt horrendously guilty for the little blossoming spark of pride and pleasure that the acknowledgement evoked.

'I don't know what you're doing here,' Sander murmured cruelly, and it was cruel because he believed that she had contacted him again because she had thought better of her headstrong decision to ditch him out of hand. His attention pinned to her, he veiled his gaze, but not before he had noticed the proud swell of her beautiful breasts and recalled the strawberry flavour of her succulent mouth. Willing his libido back under control, Sander looked directly at her, mentally censoring out his awareness of her most sexy attributes.

'Well, it's nothing to do with what happened at the club that night,' Tally declared straight off, keen to make that point for the sake of her pride. 'You behaved badly and I've got nothing to add to what I said in my text!'

A surge of irate colour accentuated the hard line of Sander's cheekbones and his golden eyes positively flashed at the schoolmistressy tone she had utilised on him. 'You acted like a drama queen.'

'No, your behaviour didn't give me a choice. A drama queen would've made a scene there and then. I chose not to,' Tally pointed out, staring back at him and registering that he was rigid with anger and scarcely able to credit that she was daring to challenge him again. But she wasn't surprised he was furious because she had only truly realised that evening at the club that Sander had probably often got away with treating women badly. He was very rich and very good-looking and very much in demand. Easy come, easy go. New, exciting lovers were always on offer to him. Many of those women doubtless took whatever he dished out, eager to please and hold his attention at any cost, but that was not Tally's way.

Strong and proud as she was, Tally was constitutionally incapable of overlooking the kiss Sander had shared with Oleia Telis unless he was able to excuse or explain it in some way, but it was obvious that Sander was in no mood to offer any explanation of his conduct. However, the recollection of his behaviour still cut through Tally like a knife, hurting like hell.

'You walked out on me just because Oleia was flirting with me. She was far from sober and she's one of my oldest friends.'

'I didn't see you pushing her away.'

The wilful curve of his wide sensual mouth had never been more obvious. 'I'm not a eunuch and you don't own me.'

'No, I don't,' Tally agreed in an attempt to draw the aggression he exuded out of the atmosphere; it was doing neither of them any favours. 'But that's not why I asked you to see me...'

'You want me back,' Sander pronounced with unassailable assurance and the urge to slap him grew so unbearable that her hand actually tingled with longing.

'No, *no*, I don't,' Tally insisted and she knew she was lying because, in spite of everything, including the fact that she was furious with him, she *did* want him back. The gentler side of her nature accepted that she still loved Sander and wanted to be with him, but reason intervened to crush such inexcusable thoughts to dust. *Not unless he grovelled*, and she knew Sander well enough to know that grovelling was not on the cards.

'So, what are you doing here?' Sander enquired with the galling air of a male who knew exactly where she was coming from and, for an instant, she felt as guilty as though the conception were entirely her fault because he had no idea what she was about to tell him.

Tally sucked in a jagged breath that jarred her taut throat muscles. 'I'll come straight to the point. I saw my doctor yesterday. I've just discovered that I'm pregnant.'

The ensuing silence spread like an oil slick, heavy, suffocating and dark.

'How pregnant?' Sander finally asked baldly.

'About six weeks,' Tally advanced breathlessly.

Sander gazed straight back at her from below spiky black lashes, his expression blank, though the pallor of shock spread visibly beneath his bronzed complexion. From the instant she'd delivered her text, he'd accepted that their relationship was over for good and now he felt utterly betrayed. 'Clearly it was a mistake for me to trust you to such an extent.'

'I didn't wilfully arrange for this to happen, Sander,' Tally protested in an emotional surge, her green eyes full of concern and distress. 'I *was* guilty of assuming that there was no risk of pregnancy from the instant I started taking contraceptive pills. I confess I didn't even read the leaflet I was given—I thought I knew it all already.' She grimaced expressively at her stupidity. 'It took my GP to explain that certain things can reduce the effectiveness of the pill and—'

'You're wasting your breath. If you're pregnant I can join up the dots for myself. Conception 101,' Sander derided, his raw indignation etched in the tautness of his strong facial bones and the edge of his intonation. 'I also assume that you're planning to have this baby.'

'Yes.'

'Naturally.'

Sensitive to his tone, Tally stiffened defensively. 'And what's that supposed to mean?'

'That raising my child gives you the excuse

to live at my expense for the best part of the next twenty years, so naturally you will want to go ahead and give birth,' Sander extended with barely concealed scorn. 'Conceiving my child was an astute financial move to make, a definite investment in the future.'

Her face flamed as though he had slapped her. Contempt and cynicism had licked round every syllable of that little speech. 'We both took risks, Sander. Believe me, I didn't plan this and I abhor the idea of living at your expense for the next twenty years!' she slung back at him with unhidden resentment.

'A rich man is always a target for this kind of scam—'

'This is not a scam. For the last time, this is not some sort of attempt to defraud you of your hard-earned cash!' Tally launched at him wrathfully. 'It was an accident and right now I'm not any happier about my having conceived than you are. After all, this baby is going to have a much bigger impact on my life than on yours!'

'I trusted you,' Sander grated, hard dark eyes

welded to her in condemnation, and it was clear that he had not accepted a word she had said as truth. 'I should have known better. A girl from my own world would have too much class to pull a stunt like this!'

'Who the heck do you think you are to speak to me like that?' So much angry resentment was roaring up through Tally that she could hardly contain it and that snobbish crack about her more humble station in life was the last straw. 'Your assumptions about me are *so* wrong. My parents broke up while my mother was pregnant and I never really had a relationship with my father because there was so much bad feeling between them. I'm the last woman in the world who would want to have a child in similar circumstances because I know the damage that growing up without a father did to me.'

'Obviously I will do what is right for you and the child and support you both,' Sander ground out with grim finality. 'Of course I will.'

'Damn you…' Tally gasped strickenly, pierced to the heart by his businesslike attitude towards an issue as deeply personal as their future child. 'It doesn't have to be like this between us. You should know me well enough to know that I would never have planned this.'

Sander raised a sleek ebony brow, dark golden eyes still smouldering with displeasure and suspicion 'Should I? I didn't think you would surprise me with news like this but I was wrong on that score. What else might I have got wrong about you?'

Devastated by that admission of distrust, Tally felt her eyes sting and she opened them very wide to hold back the tears. 'Only a few days ago we were happy—'

'And now we're not. That's life,' Sander cut her short with a sardonic bite that tore her sentimental comment to shreds. 'I do appreciate that you came here to give me this news face to face. But if you've said all you need to say I can't see that we have anything more to discuss at the moment. The legal firm I use here in London will handle this situation for me. I will pass on your details and they will be in touch.'

Tally was devastated by his outlook and the very obvious fact that he was determined to keep her at arm's length. 'I thought that I knew you better than this.'

'You knew I didn't want a child or even a serious girlfriend right from the start of our affair,' Sander reminded her without hesitation.

'Sometimes life trips you up...sometimes it's nobody's fault when things don't go the way you planned them,' Tally countered, enraged that he was blaming her for a development that she would never have willingly chosen. 'But the unexpected—the baby—will only be a disaster if we make it one—'

'Save the cheesy platitudes for someone who will welcome them,' Sander advised with icy hauteur. 'My lawyer will contact you.'

Pale as death, Tally walked back to the door. 'I don't appreciate being treated like some kind of confidence trickster.'

'And I don't appreciate being forced into becoming a father,' Sander retorted in a flat rejoinder.

* * *

A week after that encounter, Sander was surprised to learn from his PA that Anatole Karydas had demanded a meeting with him.

Although his father often did business through Anatole—for Anatole was a renowned mover and shaker—Sander had only met the older man in passing and he didn't like what he knew about Anatole's dodgy business methods. Anatole was, however, a very influential wheeler-dealer with fingers in lots of different pies. He was also a notoriously bad-tempered bully, feared by his employees and his competitors for never forgetting a mistake or a slight.

'Volakis...' Anatole grunted in acknowledgement as he came in, a small portly figure with sharp dark eyes and an unmistakeable air of pomposity. 'I believe you met my daughter at Westgrave Manor a couple of months ago.'

'I gave Cosima a lift home one evening,' Sander acknowledged with care, wondering if that was Anatole's notion of small talk.

'Tally told me that you played the Good Samaritan,' Anatole commented, watching Sander frown in surprise at that reference. 'Although I choose not to make a song and dance about it, Tally Spencer happens to be my daughter as well.'

Sander stared fixedly at the older man, convinced he must have misunderstood. 'Sorry, Tally is…also your *daughter*?'

'I never married her mother, of course, and my wife and Cosima don't want the relationship acknowledged. To be frank, I've never had much to do with Tally. I can't stand her harpy of a mother,' Anatole revealed with a curled lip. 'But Tally's still my blood and I won't stand by in silence and allow you to wreck her life.'

If Tally had been standing there at that instant, Sander truly believed he would have strangled her for concealing her true identity from him. Indeed, from the moment they had met, she had deliberately deceived him by pretending that she worked for her half-sister, Cosima. He was beginning to appreciate that he had never known Tally Spencer at all. A male unaccustomed to the discomfiture of being taken very much by surprise, Sander felt his temper blaze up beneath his controlled surface.

'Obviously you're aware that Tally is carrying my child. I hope I haven't wrecked anybody's life,' Sander murmured drily. 'I don't turn my back on my responsibilities, Anatole, and I will support Tally in every way possible.'

'You get my daughter pregnant, you marry her,' Anatole contradicted without hesitation. 'As far as I'm concerned, any other form of support is an insult to me and my family name.'

Shocked though he was by that speech, Sander could feel a current of icy self-restraint spreading through him, a current powered by the shrewd and cautious genes of his aristocratic ancestors. Anatole's vulgarity and his attempt to interfere were distasteful but it was not surprising that so self-important a man should have chosen to regard Tally's situation as a personal affront to his dignity.

'No insult was intended.'

Already tiring of the conversation, Anatole took a belligerent step forward and shook a clenched fist. 'Either you marry my girl or I pull the rug out from beneath your father.'

Sander froze. 'What are you saying?'

'That, whether you know it or not, Volakis Shipping is dangerously over-extended. Your late brother borrowed and spent too much for a business trading in an economic crisis. Your father needs to win the TKR contract to keep your family company solvent,' Anatole outlined with a bullish expression. 'If I speak a word in the wrong quarter, that contract will be awarded elsewhere and Volakis Shipping will go down.'

Sander studied Anatole with revulsion. He was well aware that the family shipping firm was over extended. In funding an expansion at the wrong time, his late brother Titos had taken too many risks in a field where competition was fierce and prices keen. Sander had no doubt that it was within Anatole's power to kill the TKR contract dead with just the whisper that Volakis Shipping might be a risky choice of carrier. Guilt assailed him. He had ignored his suspicion that his father, Petros, was struggling to handle more than he was equipped to deal with, and that sense of responsibility only grew as Sander recognised how much his own unlucky dalliance with Tally might ultimately cost his family.

'I have to consider this,' Sander breathed between clenched teeth, his self-discipline stretched thin because he would have been happier to plant a fist in Anatole's smug face. 'Did Tally tell you that she was pregnant?'

'Her mother did,' Anatole admitted harshly. 'Tally has no idea I'm here.'

The older man took his leave. Sander was in a daze, the foundations of his world in a state of collapse. He was expected to marry her? Marry Tally Spencer…Karydas? Sander wanted to punch the wall in furious frustration. He felt… *trapped*. He didn't want to get married. He had once, as a naïve teenager, wanted to marry Oleia but that dream had gone sour overnight, never to be revisited. He had learned a lot from that disillusionment, although clearly not as much as he believed, he conceded bitterly.

Tally had made a very good job of fooling him. An ordinary girl? He suppressed a contemptuous laugh. Self-evidently, there was nothing ordinary about Tally, who had gone out of her way to conceal her true parentage from him. But it hadn't taken her long to show her real colours and wheel out the big guns in the shape of her thuggish father. How could anyone expect him to believe that she had not personally informed Anatole of her condition? An accidental pregnancy? How could he ever credit that story now? Anatole Karydas was as crafty and calculating as a man could be and it looked very much as though Tally had inherited more than her lack of height from her paternal genes.

Anatole Karydas was blackmailing him. Sander ground his even white teeth together in disbelief. *Marry Tally or else.* And Sander would have called Anatole's bluff, had it not been for the fact that it would be his parents, rather than himself, who would pay the price for his refusal to give way to the older man's demand. He was already uncomfortably aware that, in recent years, he had been a less than dutiful son and although he had never been close to his parents, he still loved them and cared about what happened to them.

Sander knew that he could survive the fall of Volakis Shipping unscathed. He did not depend for support either on his parents or on the family business. But he was painfully conscious that six generations of his family had sweated blood and tears to build that business into a world-renowned shipping line. In the space of three years his older brother had destroyed an established concern with his grandiose determination to modernise and expand almost overnight. Sander's parents would be devastated if they lost the company, not to mention the comfortable lifestyle and society status that they took for granted.

There was no way that Sander could allow that to happen to them at their stage in life...no way at all. He was their son and there were bonds that even the strongest rebel could not deny. He could not stand by and watch Volakis Shipping fail simply to retain his own freedom and independence.

And Tally was, it had to be said, his every fantasy in bed, he mused with reflective heat. That was one plus, though the baby she was carrying was a very big minus on his terms. Sander could barely credit that he had run such a huge risk on the contraceptive front merely to enjoy the freedom of sex without a protective barrier. Why the hell had he done that? After all, he hated the idea of becoming a father, indeed had never been drawn to that prospect. Babies cried and pooped and smelled, and he had always seen them as a very unattractive option. When they grew into toddlers they threw tantrums and food and made incessant demands, and their unappealing habits only became more pronounced and disruptive with age. Even worse, he had noticed that wives tended to concentrate their energies on their children rather than on their husbands. A baby…the very thought of such an entity upsetting his carefree and unashamedly self-indulgent life turned Sander cold. He supposed that he wouldn't be expected to have very much to do with it. A good nanny, a *team* of good nannies, would make all the difference to their lives, he told himself in mounting desperation.

Marriage… Sander poured himself a stiff drink and tipped it back with scant appreciation. He knew that he was going to get very, very drunk before he went to see Tally the next day. He dared not mention her father's visit. Suppressing his anger on that issue, he reminded himself that, having been brutally honest with her when she told him about the baby, he now had fences to mend. He also had an honourable proposal to make in response to the most dishonourable act of blackmail...

CHAPTER EIGHT

BEING no fan of those who wallowed in misery to drama-queen depths, Tally gave herself only twenty-four hours to come to terms with the worst of Sander's absolute rejection.

He had told her no lies, Tally conceded then, struggling to be fair, even though his reaction to her news had torn her to shreds. Right from the start Sander had spelt out his position on commitment and his loathing for unplanned conceptions. But the sheer level of his angry bitterness and distrust had still come as a nasty surprise. His determination to have nothing more to do with her on a personal basis only reminded her that their child would be an ongoing financial responsibility that he would be less able to avoid. Was he planning to behave as *her* reluctant father had behaved? Would their child in turn become

Sander's youthful mistake and dirty little secret? Did he truly believe that Tally could be eagerly anticipating a future to be lived at his expense?

Yet, wasn't that in many ways what her own mother had done? a little voice asked Tally, and she almost cringed at that deeply embarrassing but unavoidable comparison. It was a fact that Crystal had stopped any pretence of working for a living after finally being awarded child maintenance in court. Nor could Tally deny the existence of women willing to conceive a child either in an attempt to hold onto a man or as a means of gaining an income. The most obvious difference between mother and daughter was that Crystal had planned her pregnancy while assuming that the father of her child would marry her. Sadly, her mother's pungent disappointment at the way in which her hopes and dreams had come to nothing had not abated with the passage of time and Tally wanted no part of such bitterness. By the time she reached her forties she didn't want to still be agonising over a rejection that had occurred in her youth.

That fact acknowledged, however, Tally had

cried until her eyes were raw. She had lost the man she loved at the same time as she was forced to accept that thanks to her condition he could hardly wait to banish her from his life. His lack of care and concern, not to mention his suspicions about her character, had hurt her a great deal.

'Realistically,' Crystal said drily the following week when Tally was calm enough to discuss things without breaking down, 'what more did you expect from Sander Volakis when you went to see him?'

Tally looked across the breakfast bar at her mother and compressed her soft mouth. 'I really did think that he cared about me...not true love but, you know, *cared*,' she stressed with genuine pain in her unhappy eyes. 'But when I told him about the baby I might as well have been some girl he slept with one night and forgot about afterwards.'

Crystal frowned. 'You can be so naïve, Tally. If you think about it, Sander was only with you because he was having fun...and very few men, if any, see a baby as a fun extra. It's not what he signed up for.'

'I suppose not,' Tally conceded gruffly, resisting a dangerous urge to admit that it wasn't what she had signed up for either. But if she took that stance, Crystal would again start discussing adoption or termination as possible options to her dilemma. Her mother had said she would back her daughter regardless of what she chose to do. While Tally appreciated that support, she was already sufficiently scared of the future without listening to Crystal tell her yet again how much having a child had impacted on *her* life and spoilt it by stealing her freedom and scaring off eligible men. It astonished Tally that she and her mother could have such different memories of her childhood.

'But at least Sander didn't try to deny responsibility and he's already promised that he'll cover the bills—he's streets ahead of your father in that line,' Crystal pronounced with a level of contempt for Anatole that could only make her daughter wince.

With her final exams coming up, Tally did not

have the luxury of sitting about talking or of staring into space and feeling wretched. She retired to her room to study, aware that with a child on the way it was even more important that she gain the qualifications she needed to find work. It was towards the end of that week that her phone rang and she was startled when she realised that it was actually Sander calling her again.

'We need to talk some more,' Sander breathed the instant she answered, his dark accented drawl level and expressionless. 'I'll pick you up at eight—'

'No,' Tally broke in hastily, keen to ensure that he did not run into her mother but not even hesitating over whether or not to agree to see him again. 'There's no need. I'll meet you—where?'

He suggested his apartment and although she would have preferred surroundings that would not awaken memories of happier times she knew they could only discuss her pregnancy in privacy. But what could he possibly want to talk about? The stance he had taken at his office had been so unqualified, so final, that it had left no room for compromise. Her curiosity was intense but he gave no hints as to why he wanted to see her again during that brief, almost businesslike call.

The front door was open for her arrival and she breathed in deep, smoothing damp palms down over the filmy top she wore teamed with a short skirt. The only special effort she had made with her appearance had gone into eradicating the evidence of tears and a sleepless night from her face but even so, with all her defensive antenna in place and her head held high, her heart was beating so fast she wanted to press a hand against her breastbone to slow it down.

Sander had only one agenda in mind: to do what had to be done and move on. He had dealt with setbacks before and, at ease with taking charge of difficult situations, he always forged boldly ahead. But when Tally walked in, other responses took over. He noticed the new wariness in her lack of facial expression and cautious entrance. The happy glow and smiles he was accustomed to receiving were gone. Nor, now that he knew the facts that she should never have kept from him, could he rise above the need to see if he could trace her parentage in her looks.

Hostility licked through him when he found himself instinctively linking her lack of height and slightly prominent nose to Anatole Karydas' paternity.

Tally focused on Sander's lean powerful figure and tried and failed to swallow. She was horribly short of breath. His superb cheekbones were taut below his bronzed skin. He was a devastatingly handsome guy and he still made her tummy flip and her mouth run dry in knee-jerk reactions she could not suppress, but the fierce tension in the air could only increase her discomfiture.

'Would you like a drink?' he asked politely.

'No, thanks.' In an effort to seem in control, Tally parked herself on the edge of a leather sofa, knees pinned together, handbag at her feet. In the pool of lamplight her tumbling mane of corkscrew curls acquired a glowing amber vibrancy while the see-through quality of her top was accentuated. Momentarily, his cold dark gaze rested on the voluptuous curves spilling over beneath the fine fabric of her bra and a hunger he despised assailed him. Swiftly he redirected his attention to the anxious green eyes locked to his lean strong face.

Anger flared in Sander at that look, although he was not at all surprised that she was worried. She had told him outright lies and kept secrets from him and he was now fully convinced that she must've set him up as a fall guy for her pregnancy. He was not slow on the uptake and since Anatole's visit he had made enquiries, learning enough about Tally's background in the process to marvel at the parallels between the circumstances of her birth and her current condition. And Sander had never believed in innocent coincidences.

'You said we needed to talk some more,' Tally prompted tightly, her nerves jumping, diving and weaving like acrobats in the strained silence.

'Last week, you took me by surprise and I'm afraid I didn't react very well to your announcement,' Sander drawled in a smooth-as-silk opener.

Wondering where the dialogue was going, Tally closed her trembling fingers together to steady them. 'No, you didn't,' she agreed. 'But

I know that what I had to tell you must've come as a shock.'

'But, as you said, it doesn't follow that the advent of a child has to be seen as a disaster,' Sander delivered, tipping his drink to his mouth and using alcohol to force sentiments that tasted false from his mouth. He was twenty-five years old and he wasn't ready for a baby in his life. He had nothing against babies, he just didn't want one of his own, not for years and years and years, if at all. Furthermore lying wasn't his way. Telling the truth and shaming the devil came much more naturally to him but he did not want to risk confronting Tally with his suspicions before they were safely married. He could not afford to jeopardise the future of Volakis Shipping. He gritted his even white teeth on the crushing conviction that he did not have a choice as to what he did next. Anatole Karydas had taken free choice out of the equation and put family loyalty squarely in its place.

'It would be much better if we could be civilised about this situation,' Tally remarked, thinking unhappily of the bitter animosity that still flourished between her parents even after the passage of so many years.

'I have every intention of doing the best I can for you and the baby,' Sander asserted. 'That may surprise you after the way I behaved.'

'No, it doesn't surprise me,' Tally interrupted with a shadow of her once sunny smile that sought to dispel the fierce tension in the room. 'You're not an irresponsible person, you're just volatile and you were angry. I understood that.'

Disconcerted by the manner in which she pronounced judgement on his character with a familiarity that no other woman had ever dared to employ, Sander drained his glass and set it down with a decisive snap. 'I want you to marry me,' he told her, and because he *needed* her to marry him to save Volakis Shipping the proposal fell from his lips with all the convincing gravitas of the perfect truth.

Astonishment made Tally's eyes fly wide. She was deeply shaken, for that proposal was just about the last thing she had expected to hear from him. Paralysed into stillness, she stared, her eyes dark as emeralds and full of confusion and uncertainty. 'Are you serious?'

'Wouldn't it be a very stupid thing to say if I wasn't?'

Embarrassment washed colour back into Tally's cheeks and beaded perspiration on her short upper lip. She was wildly flustered and trying to hide it. With an effort she straightened her slight shoulders and looked back at him again. 'But you know you don't *really* want to marry me, Sander, so it would be the wrong thing to do.'

Taken aback by that unexpected response, Sander frowned, his ebony brows drawing together. 'I *do* want to marry you,' he said again.

The tip of Tally's tongue slipped out to moisten her dry lower lip. A heightened state of excitement was making her heart thump in what felt like the foot of her throat. She wanted to snatch at his proposal with both hands and name the day. After all, she loved him and he was offering her most secret dream, the for ever relationship she had believed until now could only exist in her own imagination. But it still felt more like a dream than reality and the last thing she wanted from Sander was a proposal made only on the basis of her pregnancy because she was convinced that a marriage in which he unwillingly surrendered his freedom could never survive.

'At the end of the day, the baby won't care whether we're married or not,' she pointed out gently. 'And we haven't been together for long enough to be talking about getting married. You're only suggesting marriage because I'm pregnant.'

Brilliant dark eyes gleaming, Sander said in dry challenge, 'Is there something wrong with that? In my family, we get married *before* we have children and any other remedy is unacceptable to me.'

Tally flushed to the roots of her hair at that rejoinder. He knew her parents were unmarried and was making it clear that he was from a rather more conventional family set-up. 'I just don't want you asking me to marry you because of the baby. That's not enough to sustain a relationship and it's not your style either. You like your freedom.'

Sander wondered if she was deliberately

mocking him or if he was supposed to be impressed and touched by her apparent reluctance to become his wife in such circumstances. 'Of course I like my freedom but I have decided that I would like you in my bed every night even more.'

That unashamedly blunt admission sent a scorching wave of heat travelling through Tally's taut length. Meeting his smouldering dark golden gaze, Tally felt the pulse beat of desire kick low in her pelvis and create a mortifying tingle of awareness between her legs. 'But only ten days ago it seemed to be Oleia Telis whom you wanted in your bed,' she reminded him unhappily.

'It's more than five years since I last slept with Oleia and I can assure you that I have no intention of resurrecting that relationship,' Sander declared without hesitation.

'But obviously you still find her attractive,' Tally responded uneasily, dismayed by the evident fact that his ties with the tiny brunette stretched back that far and had, indeed, once been as intimate as she had feared.

'No, *she* still finds me attractive,' Sander corrected with arrogant cool. 'It's a rather perverse game that we play. Let me explain. When I was twenty I was very much in love with Oleia, but she shagged another guy and I ditched her. She's been trying to get me back ever since but I could never forgive what she did.'

Tally felt the emotional punch of what he was telling her, recognising the truth when she heard it in the roughened edge to his dark deep drawl and the grimness briefly etched in his lean dark features. Once upon a time he had loved Oleia and she had betrayed him and her infidelity had hurt him badly. Tally knew his dark temperament well enough to grasp that Oleia's ongoing eager pursuit would appeal to his desire to settle the score and soothe his male ego.

'So, it amuses you to let Oleia come on to you and kiss you,' Tally remarked thinly.

Sander gazed levelly back at her. 'I never thought about it. It was nothing, it meant nothing, it was going nowhere. I didn't know you were watching my every move or that you would be so narrow-minded.'

Tally's fingers closed into defensive fists. She

had finally got an explanation about Oleia and she didn't want to waste time getting into an argument with him on that score. He had told her the unlovely truth about Oleia and she appreciated that, but time had moved on and she had more important things to worry about, not least the baby she carried.

'If I'm narrow-minded, it's with good reason,' Tally countered heavily. 'I just don't approve of people being too free and easy when it comes to sex. That's basically why I grew up without a father.'

Sander's lean, darkly handsome features were taut. 'But Anatole still regards you as his daughter...'

It was Tally's turn to freeze in surprise. 'You already know that Anatole Karydas is my father? I never really saw the point of mentioning it because he takes so little to do with me. But how did you find out?'

'He told me,' Sander fielded flatly, his expressive mouth compressing on the grudging admission. 'He also admitted that his wife and Cosima didn't like people knowing you existed.'

Relieved that the secret was out, even though she was surprised that her father should have confided in him, Tally muttered, 'Cosima didn't want anyone to know the truth. She insisted on pretending that I worked for her that weekend at Westgrave. How did you meet Anatole?'

'Your father does business with mine.' As he was in no position to challenge her story or reveal his true feelings, Sander compressed his handsome mouth and returned to his most pressing objective. 'I want to marry you as soon as it can be arranged—'

'But *why*?' Tally asked him helplessly. 'You don't love me.'

'I want you more than I've wanted any woman in a very long time and that physical connection is very important to me,' Sander breathed thickly, black lashes low over his molten golden gaze as he studied her with a sexual heat she could literally feel. 'Right now I just want to cut through all this bull and take you back to bed…'

Her nipples straining into prominence beneath her clothes, Tally experienced a hollow ache at the heart of her and she went pink, acknowledging the power of the fiery sexual hunger that still drew them together even as she was moved to protest, 'People don't marry just to share a bed.'

'Why not? I marry you and I take care of you and the baby. What could be more normal?'

Being taken care of was a seductive proposition for a young woman who had had to fight to get any attention from either of her parents as a child. 'But would that be enough for you?'

'Why shouldn't it be?' Sander responded. 'Why are you making this so complicated?'

'I don't want either of us to make a mistake,' Tally confided ruefully, fighting her desire to say yes and let him drag her off to bed then and there. 'When we met at your office, you didn't seem to want anything to do with me or the baby.'

'But now I've adjusted to your announcement and I recognise that this is my baby as well,' Sander countered levelly.

That declaration impressed her. 'But you were *so* angry with me.'

'That was unjust.' Sander shifted a broad shoulder in a dismissive gesture. 'As I didn't use condoms I'm as much to blame for this development as you are.'

'If you really believe that I could be the wife you want, I'll marry you,' Tally framed awkwardly, wishing that she could just throw herself into his arms and wondering why on earth she should still feel so uneasy about his proposal. Was it that it seemed too good to be true that she loved him and had fallen pregnant and he should want to marry her?

'Okay, so we'll get the deed done as quickly as possible,' Sander pronounced impatiently, in no mood to dress up the occasion with fine words or gestures. 'Next week would suit my schedule—'

'Next week?' Tally parroted in pure disbelief. 'I'm about to start my final exams and it'll be two weeks before I've finished.'

'I don't think it will take long to organise a quiet civil ceremony.'

Tally stiffened and sent him a rueful glance. 'I would rather get married in church, Sander. It could still be small and quiet.'

His beautifully shaped mouth compressed with an impatience he could not hide. 'If you say so. I don't really care how we go about it, I just want it staged as soon as possible.'

Tally had read that men were rarely enthusiastic about wedding arrangements. But why was such haste necessary? It would be quite a few weeks before her condition became obvious. Was he embarrassed by the prospect of a visibly pregnant bride? Or a baby who would be born less than the requisite nine months after the wedding? Sander was too much his own man for her to credit either possibility.

'Look, maybe we should both spend a couple of days thinking this over before we rush into anything,' Tally suggested, her common sense winning out over her reluctance to allow him another opportunity to consider his position.

Sander frowned, dark as night eyes flashing with angry intolerance. 'But you said you would marry me.'

'Yes, and I absolutely *meant* it!' Tally broke in with a passionate vehemence she could not restrain. 'But this is a complete turnaround for you and it worries me that you're in such a hurry.'

Sander released his breath in a hiss, dangerous

golden eyes locked in seething challenge to her troubled face. 'I don't know what more you want from me.'

Tally wondered if she was being hugely unfair and foolish. After all, she wanted his heart and it wasn't on offer. Oleia had evidently planted a dainty but destructive stiletto heel in that organ when he was at an impressionable age and the women who had followed in her footsteps had reaped the distrust, cynicism and emotional detachment that Oleia had sown.

'I need to know that you truly want a life with me and our child and that this isn't some crazy impulse which you will regret in a few months' time.'

His beautiful wilful mouth took on a sardonic slant. 'Do you think I know myself so little? Or is it simply that you're offended that I didn't do the big proposal scene?'

'It is only a week since you told me to take my cheesy platitudes and pretty much get out of your office!' Tally slammed back at him as she grabbed up her bag and sprang upright, eager to take her leave before her simmering emotions led her into an argument she did not want to have.

Alive with wrathful impatience and frustration, Sander closed his lean hands over hers and pulled her up against him, hot golden eyes hungrily raking her flushed and unhappy face. He shifted his lean hips and she tensed when she felt the thrusting urgency of his arousal even through his clothing. 'Let's forget the talking. It's getting us nowhere. Come to bed,' he breathed thickly.

And the hot shivery desire that shot like a sheet of flame through Tally in response to that blunt invitation left no part of her untouched. Her nipples peaked, her breasts swelled and heat and damp gathered between her thighs. She wanted to say yes, she wanted to say yes so badly that the very word was on her lips because she knew that sexual intimacy would ease the terrible tension and allow her to feel close to him again. She was eager for the proof that he still found her desirable, for only that could make her feel in any way secure when he didn't love her. But on a more rational level she was experiencing a sixth-sense feeling of apprehension that would not let her alone and turned the fever in her blood cold.

'I think it would be better if I went straight home tonight,' Tally contended, pulling back from him with strained eyes as she fought the craving he always evoked in her. She did not know how to explain the feelings afflicting her, she only knew that she did not want to add a bout of wild make-up sex to an already volatile situation. She was very much afraid that, willing partner though she would be, sex would only make her feel used because what she really wanted from him just then were reassuring words and feelings, rather than the mindless excitement of his lovemaking. And there was really no point expecting him to deliver the more tender emotions he was not experiencing.

Swinging away from her in receipt of the rare rejection, Sander raked long fingers through his cropped black hair and swore under his breath before breathing rawly, 'I assumed we would be celebrating.'

'My hormones are all over the place at the minute,' Tally muttered apologetically. 'The last week has been pretty traumatic and I need some down time to think and revise for my exams.'

'I just don't know where you're coming from—'

'Let's fix a date for the wedding,' Tally broke in, her desperation mounting and she shifted closer and stretched up to kiss the corner of his mouth in a soothing gesture of affection.

Unfortunately the gesture failed to work its magic. Sander closed his hands into the torrent of her curls and he held her fast while he plundered her mouth with a dark driving need that speared through her like a lightning bolt. Even so she still wouldn't surrender to her hunger and she fell back from him, her ripe mouth red and swollen. Eyes cloaked, he gazed down at her moodily and noticed with an unexpected sense of satisfaction that when she smiled dizzily up at him, her dimples were showing again.

'Three weeks today,' Tally bargained, keen to smooth away the tension still hardening his lean, dark, devastatingly handsome features. 'Three weeks today we get married... Okay?'

When she had gone in the taxi he had procured and paid for, Sander reminded himself sardonically that at least on one level he had got what he wanted. Was it too cynical to suspect that she had decided to withhold the voluptuous delights of her curvy little body until she got that wedding ring on her finger? Had the natural candid girl who had initially attracted him only existed in his own imagination? It was a depressing suspicion.

Unusually, Crystal got out of bed to see her daughter when she got home and Tally wasted no time in sharing her news. 'Sander's asked me to marry him and we're thinking of three weeks today if it can be arranged.'

Crystal's face lit up as though someone had switched on a floodlight inside her and she hugged her daughter in a rare display of physical affection. 'That's wonderful, darling! It'll be a challenge to organise a wedding that fast, but I agree that it would be unwise to wait any longer. Look at what happened to me!'

Tally resisted the temptation to remark that her mother had been the leading light in her own downfall and quietly removed cups from a cupboard to make tea. 'If Sander does change his mind, I won't hold it against him. Marriage is a very big step.'

'So is having a baby. Why *should* Sander change his mind?' Crystal demanded sharply as she withdrew a bottle of vodka from another cupboard. 'No, don't make me tea. I'm going to celebrate this news with something stronger.'

'You'll probably think I'm being stupid but I really don't want Sander to feel that he *has* to marry me because I'm pregnant,' Tally confided in a rush.

'What does it matter?' Crystal countered impatiently and then a Cheshire cat grin flashed across her mouth again. 'Oh, darling, I can't *believe* you've actually pulled it off!'

Tally's brow furrowed. 'Pulled what off?'

'You've caught yourself a multi-millionaire and you're going to be a respectably married wife. I never got to be a wife!' her mother pointed out bitterly. 'I never got the big wedding either, but you're going to—'

'Sander doesn't want a big wedding and he doesn't want anyone to know about the baby yet,' Tally cut in uncomfortably, wishing the older woman weren't quite so impressed by Sander's wealth but rather touched by her excitement. 'Mum, I was really shocked when he proposed and I'm worried that he hasn't really thought it through.'

For an instant, Crystal fell oddly still and veiled her eyes. 'That's silly. Why do you always look for problems?'

'I just don't think I'm sufficiently beautiful or important enough to marry someone like Sander,' Tally told her with pained honesty. 'He's gorgeous and rich and very successful—'

'And he's the father of your child, so you *deserve* a ring!' Crystal interrupted forcefully. 'Why should you struggle for years to bring a kid up on your own?'

'Lots of other women do.'

'I want you to have what I never got!' the older woman declared emotively.

In the days that followed Tally focused on her revision for her final exams and distracted by Sander taking off on a business trip to Brazil and only rarely phoning her, eventually realised in dismay that her mother was living her dream rather than *her* daughter's. Once Anatole had been told about the forthcoming nuptials—though not yet about the baby—Tally's father had confirmed that he would foot all the bills, even though he would not be attending his daughter's wedding. Crystal hired a top-flight wedding planner and went into action. From that moment on, every bridal extravagance seemed to be in the pipeline, including the appearance of two cousins Tally barely knew to act as bridesmaids in concert with a school friend. In vain did Tally remonstrate with the elaborate arrangements her headstrong parent was making. Even so, it did not occur to her that there might be more widespread repercussions until Sander turned up unannounced at the house the week before the wedding.

'I didn't know you were back in London.' In answer to Binkie's call, Tally came downstairs. She wished she had known he was coming because she was murderously uncomfortable, greeting him clad in comfortable track pants and a shapeless sweatshirt.

Predictably, Sander looked amazing in a

sharply cut navy designer suit and a blue and white striped shirt. His strong jaw line roughened with dark stubble, he trained his dark deep set eyes on her, metallic gold dancing like fiery sparks in his irate gaze, his stunning cheekbones taut below his bronzed skin.

'What's wrong?' Tally prompted instantly, tension gripping her.

'I believe you had a Save the Date card and a request for a guest list of two hundred people sent to my parents last week—they didn't even know I was getting married!' he launched at her in wrathful condemnation. 'They've only just chosen to tell me.'

Tally settled aghast eyes on his lean strong face. 'You still haven't told your parents about us?'

In the face of her disbelief, Sander's lean muscular frame went rigid. 'It not the sort of announcement you make on the phone. I'm flying home this evening to speak to them.'

'You should've told them the minute we set the date,' Tally countered defensively, demoralised by his admission that he had yet to discuss his marital plans with his parents. Was he ashamed of her? Or simply trying to forget the fact that he would soon be a married man with a wife and a child on the way?

'You didn't warn me that a virtual circus would be kicking off back here in London!' Sander slung back at her between gritted teeth. 'I told you I wanted a quiet, quick ceremony. I don't like superficial show and fuss.'

'Since you've taken absolutely no interest in anything to do with our wedding and have not asked one single question about the arrangements I can't see why it should matter to you!' Tally snapped back, the resentments she had squashed for the sake of peace now leaping out to stand toe to toe with his. 'Do you realise that it's five days since you even bothered to phone me?'

'Well, if you think I'm going to start checking in with you all the time like a truant schoolboy you're in for a big disappointment!' Sander fired back at her in glowering challenge. 'Don't start telling me what I'm supposed to be doing!'

'Would anyone like coffee?' Binkie proffered very quietly from the kitchen doorway.

'Not for me, thank you,' Sander pronounced stiffly, jerking round to acknowledge the presence of the older woman. 'I have to get to the office and catch up before I head to Athens, Tally. I doubt if I'll see you before the wedding now.'

Filled with a disappointment she was determined not to parade for his benefit, Tally folded her arms, her soft pink lips settling into a naturally mutinous pout. 'I'll survive.'

'Tally!' Binkie pronounced reproachfully as soon as the younger woman had closed the door in Sander's imperious wake. 'What's got into you?'

Tally swallowed hard and veiled her eyes, making no answer. She did not trust herself to speak. Sixth sense was sending streamers of growing apprehension sliding through her but she did not want to acknowledge her secret fears. She did not want to be forced to ask herself whether or not she ought to be marrying a guy as detached from their approaching wedding and from her as Sander currently appeared to be...

Instead, Tally listened to Binkie's comforting

conviction that few men had any patience with bridal extravaganzas, but just at the point when she was tying herself into even deeper mental knots about her bridegroom's lack of enthusiasm, a special delivery was made.

Taut with lively curiosity, Tally tore open the gift card first to stare down at Sander's signature before opening the packaging of the small parcel and extracting a jewellery box. She lifted the lid to reveal a glittering diamond ring.

In a daze of surprise, Tally slid it onto her engagement finger and then she phoned Sander, who was already on the way to the airport.

'Thank you—it's gorgeous,' she told him truthfully.

'You should ditch the exams and come out to Greece with me,' Sander responded.

That suggestion meant even more than the gift of the ring to Tally and she beamed with happiness and relief. She would have so much enjoyed accompanying him and getting the chance to meet his parents before the wedding. 'I'd have loved to do that, but I've put in three years of hard work at college and I want to graduate this year,' she told him ruefully.

Everything was really all right between them, Tally persuaded herself that night while she lay trying to get to sleep. The ring had been a thoughtful present, calculated to make her feel more like a normal bride. She needed to stop worrying and concentrate on what was really important. And what was really important was that she was about to marry the man she loved and whose child she carried, she told herself dreamily...

CHAPTER NINE

TALLY'S choice of wedding dress had been her own. While Crystal's bold ideas had reigned supreme in every other field, Tally had reserved the right to choose what she wore without interference.

For that reason, the dress wasn't the most fashionable or expensive, nor was it calculated to turn heads with its daring. While Crystal was clad in designer togs from head to toe, Tally had picked an elegant lace column with a minimal train that flattered her small shapely figure. Her short veil and beaded hair ornament were equally unfussy. In addition, although the bridesmaids rather frantically threw rose petals in the bride's path as she glided up the aisle, her mother flounced beside her in a killer silver shift dress and jacket to give her away and several flocks of doves were to be set free after the ceremony to mark the occasion, Tally exuded a wholly deceptive air of calm. Her exams were over and she was free to enjoy her day.

As she approached the altar, her outward composure was speared by warning fingers of frost when she met the cold critical appraisal of her future in-laws. Sander's well-bred parents looked as grim as if they were attending a funeral. Her heart sank at that visible vote of disapproval and anxious pink flushed her cheeks. She was grateful when Sander turned his handsome dark head to look at her and she rewarded that show of interest with a shy but appreciative beam.

Sander had the most beautiful dark golden eyes, she acknowledged dizzily, dazzled by the sheer charge of his masculine charisma. In only a few minutes, Sander would be her husband and she could still barely believe her good fortune. Although she had hardly seen him since the day she agreed to marry him, she appreciated the amount of hard work he had been doing; an upmarket business magazine had just published a profile of him, citing the entrepreneurial brilliance of his recent deals as well as the wide-scale expectation that he would shortly be taking the helm at Volakis Shipping. Reading that article, Tally was so proud of him that she had shown it to everyone she knew.

A sardonic cast to his lean strong face, Sander caught the shine in his bride's eyes and the upward tilt of her full mouth and saw that she was happy, in fact overflowing with the emotion. At least someone was in a bridal mood, he reflected wryly, thinking of the stand-up row he'd had with his father, who'd wanted him to call off the wedding rather than marry a woman he had described as 'the Karydas by-blow'. Even a reference to the baby had failed to ignite a glow of grandmotherly anticipation in his mother's eyes; in fact the older woman had referred to the advent of her first grandchild as 'the oldest trick in the book'.

On the other hand, neither of his parents had the slightest suspicion that their son might have been blackmailed into the marriage and Petros Volakis was only mildly concerned that the all-important TKR contract needed to keep the family business afloat had yet to be signed. Sander preferred his family to remain ignorant of Anatole's threats because he saw no point in revealing that he'd made a sacrifice that—if acknowledged—would only make his parents resent the hell out of his wife...or in this case resent her more than they did already.

The combined accumulation of nerves and the hormonal commotion of early pregnancy made Tally feel a little dizzy on the church steps where cameras were clicking and film whirring with the bride and groom the photographic centre of attention. As she swayed Sander closed a steadying arm round her.

'Are you feeling all right?'

'Just a tiny bit dizzy,' Tally admitted grudgingly, keen for her condition not to influence their special day in any negative way and glancing anxiously up at him as if she was ready to apologise for her uncharacteristic frailty.

Her bridegroom's lean, devastatingly handsome features tightened, his stunning dark eyes cooling, his stubborn mouth compressing, and in that single assessing glance Tally experienced a darkly unwelcome moment of insight. Sander, she recognised in dismay, definitely didn't want to be reminded that she was pregnant, or for anyone beyond the family circle to know. Maybe it was just impatience, she thought frantically, desperate to come up with a more acceptable explanation. He was young, fit and active, un-accustomed to bodily weakness. In addition, it was weeks since they had made love and he had a powerful libido. It was unlikely that he knew much about pregnancy and the hormonal and physical changes it imposed on a woman. Perhaps he was dreading the idea that his bride might turn into an ailing and untouchable preg-nant mother-to-be.

'You really will have to introduce me to your parents,' she muttered ruefully as he swung into the limo beside her. 'Do they know I'm preg-nant?'

'Of course.'

Tally tried not to feel self-conscious about the fact for, in a couple of months, people would only have to look at her to appreciate that there was a baby on the way. 'It's very awkward that I still haven't met them.'

'Between your exams and my schedule there wasn't an opportunity.' Sander watched the celebratory flock of doves take flight without wincing in disbelief and he was proud of himself for that tolerant restraint. 'But we'll both be much more accessible over the next few months. We'll be living in Athens for a while at least.'

Since he had not mentioned that salient fact before, Tally tensed. 'Are you taking over at Volakis Shipping?'

Sander nodded gravely. 'Can't avoid it any longer and I'm not sure I even want to any more. It is my family's heritage. But if my brother, Titos, hadn't died, the situation would never have arisen.'

Tally had noticed that he never mentioned his late brother. 'What was Titos like?'

'A very decent guy, clever, but he had no business brain. He and I could never have worked successfully together. He was the centre of my parents' world though.'

'They've still got you,' she pointed out gently.

Sander loosed a rather edged laugh. 'Titos fitted the bill, I never did. His death devastated them and my survival only reminds them of what they have lost.'

Tally frowned and hoped he was wrong on that score. The concept chilled her, much like the icy appraisal she had received from his parents as she walked down the aisle to marry their son. How could they not appreciate their strong and phenomenally successful younger son? Full of partisan sympathies on his behalf, she wanted to hug Sander and resisted the urge, knowing he would scorn her commiseration.

A few minutes later, the all-important intro-ductions were performed in an ante-room at the hotel where the reception was being held. Petros Volakis and his tall elegant wife, Eirene, made no attempt to welcome Tally into the family circle. The frosty atmosphere could've been cut with the proverbial knife but Sander seemed impervious to it and fell into conversation with his father several feet away. Tally switched to Greek and said, 'I speak some Greek,' to Eirene Volakis.

'I dare say your mother taught you everything

she knows,' Eirene pronounced with scorn in the same language, 'starting with the most important lesson: how to catch a rich husband with a baby. While that ploy failed her, it hasn't failed you.'

Shaken by that contemptuous response, which emphasised the unlovely fact that her in-laws knew all too many mortifying facts about her background, Tally reeled as if she had had her face slapped in public. She didn't have a bitchy bone in her body and could think of nothing to say in return, other than a rather limp, 'My mother never learned any Greek.'

As Tally moved hurriedly away Crystal grabbed her daughter's arm and whispered, 'You could freeze ice on that old trout's face! What did she say to you?'

'I think we can safely assume that I wasn't on her wish list as a daughter-in-law.'

'Don't let it upset you,' Crystal urged, although her own colour was high and it was evident she too was embarrassed by the chilly reception she had received.

Sander saw Tally's white, drawn face as she moved away from his mother. She was twisting her hands together in an uneasy movement that he had long since identified as indicative of Tally in distress mode and he immediately suspected the cause. The spasm of dark fury that ripped through him took him by surprise because he had strong reservations of his own when it came to his bride. His parents might be curling their lips in superiority at the over-the-top wedding in which bling rather than good taste ruled, but an affront to his wife was still an affront and unacceptable to Sander.

'Mum got totally carried away,' Tally told her bridegroom ruefully as she scanned the reception room, which was dominated by towering flower arrangements embellished with feathers, beading and reflective crystals, while twinkling lights winked on and off everywhere. It looked a little like a child's version of fairy land. 'I should've restrained her but she was enjoying it all so much I didn't have the heart.'

'It doesn't matter,' Sander pronounced valiantly, questioning his ability to appreciate her innate kindness and then balance that character trait with his belief that she had deliberately concealed her father's identity before pulling it out like a big gun to get him to the altar. Was she in love with him? he wondered for the first time. Was that why she had fallen pregnant? He might have chosen not to use protection but only after *she* had assured him that it would be safe. If she had trapped him out of love, was he supposed to forgive her? He did not feel forgiving, he felt like a wild animal suddenly thrown into a cage. All of a sudden, the freedom he cherished had vanished. Marriage was supposed to make him faithful and monogamous even though, to date, he had never felt the desire to be either.

The reception wore on and there was little if any mingling between the guests on the bride's side and the groom's. Without unbending in the slightest, Sander's parents left at the earliest possible moment. Tally relaxed a little and, drifting round the dance floor in Sander's strong arms, even contrived to feel dreamily happy. He held her close to his lean powerful body and her blood stirred at his proximity and the aphrodisiac scent of his skin.

Desire was slivering along her nerve endings in

a smoulderingly slow attack, when little cramping pains low in her pelvis made her tense for a different reason entirely. Without saying anything she went upstairs to the suite set aside for the bride and groom to change and there she discovered with a sinking heart that she was bleeding. In consternation she wondered if she was losing her baby and when her mother came to check on her Crystal wasted no time in using her phone to call Sander. He sought counsel from his cousin who was a doctor.

'You need medical attention,' Sander pronounced.

'But this is our wedding night!' Tally protested in dismay.

'These things happen,' Sander countered, keen to keep her calm the way his cousin had advised.

An hour and a half later, Tally was tucked into a bed in a private clinic that the doctor had recommended and the wedding day was definitely over. While Crystal had stayed on at the hotel to act as hostess, the bride had not got to throw her bouquet, stay up late at the evening party or even say goodbye to their guests. From below lowered lashes her attention was on Sander, sunk in a chair across the room, his jacket discarded and his sleeves pushed back, his stubborn jaw line now darkly shadowed by stubble. Slightly dishevelled though he was, he managed to look even more gorgeous than usual and her heart went bumpety-bumpety-bump inside her chest, leaving her breathless.

'I'm really sorry about this,' Tally whispered.

In an abrupt movement, Sander sprang upright, instantly dominating the room with his height, breadth and restlessness. He raked impatient brown fingers through his tousled black hair. 'Don't be silly—this isn't your fault.'

Tears burned the backs of her eyes in a hot surge and she blinked rapidly and hurriedly looked away, aware that the last thing he needed was an emotional scene. 'There's no point in you staying here with me. Go back to the hotel and see your friends.'

'It's two in the morning.' Sander pointed out the lateness of the hour gently, aware that she had lost track of time. 'I can't leave you here alone.'

'Why not? I'm ready to go to sleep.'

Sander shifted a shoulder in silence, expressing a concern he did not want to frame in words, his lean strong face bleak and hollow with tension. The consultant had made it clear to him that nothing more could be done to prevent her from losing the baby. If it was going to happen, it was going to happen. There was no magic cure to be applied. He did not know how he felt about the ongoing risk of a miscarriage; he just didn't want to think about it. He was more worried about Tally. He just wanted her back to her normal effervescent self; the pale, tear-stained, apologetic woman in the bed felt like a stranger.

'The staff will contact you if anything happens,' Tally muttered. 'Please go—it would make me feel better.'

In the end Sander departed, telling her that he would be back first thing in the morning. Only when Tally studied his empty chair did she let the tears flow freely. This was certainly not how she had dreamt of embarking on their shiny new marriage. She pushed her damp cheek into the pillow and tried to sleep, while trying to tell her baby to hang on in there as if her sincere good wishes could fix whatever problem there might be.

Forty-eight hours later and still pregnant, the spotting she'd been suffering having stopped, Tally left the hospital and travelled straight to the airport with her baggage to fly to Athens. Sander was already on board the private jet and spent most of the flight preoccupied with work before finally admitting that the family shipping company needed major reorganisation and that he had to hit the ground running if he was to impress his father with his commitment.

Sander owned a city apartment that was clearly designed to suit a young single male, for the kitchen was minuscule, the lounge furnished with more technology than Tally had ever seen outside a shop and the bed was huge. Recognising that his bride would be at a loose end while he was at the office, Sander suggested somewhat vaguely that she might want to visit his mother, who would introduce her to people. Tally contrived not to cringe at that piece of useless advice and bought a cookery book instead, determined to make meals that Sander would recognise.

Unfortunately her culinary efforts proved superfluous when Sander worked late every night and invariably slid into the far side of the bed in the early hours of the morning. They shared the apartment on platonic terms because he had not touched her since she had been hospitalised, a state of affairs that shook Tally; it had never crossed her mind that Sander might impose a moratorium on sex.

Finally she picked up her courage one night when he was stripping for bed in the dark, the husband who was almost becoming a stranger to her in his remoteness from her daily life and his endless working hours. 'Sander?'

'Sorry, did I wake you up?'

'I want you to wake me up. I never see you.' Tally sighed before thinking better of what might sound dangerously like a whine. 'You know, I may be pregnant but I'm totally healthy. And according to the gynaecologist at my last check-up, it's totally safe for us to make love…'

'I'm too tired tonight,' Sander delivered cuttingly, striding into the bathroom.

Cheeks flaming in the semi-darkness, Tally

almost groaned out loud and chewed at her lower lip in squirming discomfiture. Perhaps she had been clumsy. She has assumed that her threatened miscarriage had made him reluctant to initiate sex. She didn't know what else could be wrong. But then she didn't know why he was shutting her out of his life to such an extent either. He didn't talk about business or his working day, or if there were problems in either field. Worst of all was the sense she got that he was angry with her, that beneath that smooth, polite and always considerate façade of his he was like a powder keg ready to explode.

Was it her imagination that he was angry and avoiding her? She thought of the dark brooding look she had glimpsed in his stunning eyes, the clipped words and irritation, the antagonism she felt pulse in the abrupt silences that stretched even during the most casual exchanges. No, Tally was convinced that the anger was not only a figment of her imagination.

But what was Sander angry *about*? The blip in her health that had spoiled the aftermath of their wedding? The simple fact that she was pregnant and likely to become unattractively rotund in the near future? The reality that marriage could seem rather boring to a guy accustomed to frequent changes of partner? Or had he just decided that he didn't want to be with her any more? Was he only putting in his time with her until the baby was safely born?

Not so very long ago they had laughed at the same things, argued companionably and shared a terrific sexual bond but now, all of a sudden, when she was available every night he no longer seemed to find her attractive. But possibly he *was* tired, she reasoned ruefully. After all he was working incredibly long hours at Volakis Shipping and she suspected that he and his father rarely saw eye to eye, which had to be stressful and frustrating for a guy accustomed to calling all his own shots.

The following day, Tally sent Sander a text inviting him home for a meal at eight and then breaking free of her usual inhibitions, she went shopping at a lingerie boutique and stocked up on the kind of silk and lace apparel that she was convinced would appeal to any red-blooded male.

Shortly before eight she lit the candles on the table and studied herself in the mirror, grimacing a little, hugely self-conscious about the outfit she was wearing—although outfit was not an appropriate description. She was clad in a coffee and cream silk set of bra and knickers, teamed with heels, stockings and a loose chiffon wrap that revealed more than it concealed. Sander was not going to be left in any doubt of the invitation she was giving him and, on one level, her pride was mortified by the bold approach she was taking.

But the bottom line was that she loved Sander and that simple truth outweighed all other considerations, she acknowledged ruefully. She could not go on indefinitely wondering what was wrong and living on the outskirts of his life like a barely tolerated poor relation. If Sander wanted his freedom back, if he was excluding her because he resented her presence, she was better finding out now and walking away before they ended up hating each other. She had to think of their child. Her own parents, Crystal and

Anatole, loathed each other so much that they couldn't even be in the same room together. Tally was willing to do almost anything to conserve a more civilised relationship with Sander if only for their child's sake.

As the minutes marched on she had to fuss over the meal in an effort to stop it spoiling. By half-past eight she was worried; by the time he was an hour late and hadn't even phoned she was in angry tears. She did not think she had ever felt so lonely in her life as she did watching the clock tick on in the silence. She wouldn't let the tears fall and she couldn't even have a drink because she was pregnant. At ten she threw the meal in the bin and just left all the dishes sitting, then took refuge in the bedroom.

Sander let himself into the apartment just after two in the morning. Having spent a large part of the evening downing vodka with the Russian consortium who had just signed a very lucrative contract with Volakis Shipping, he was remarkably sober but almost drunk with tiredness. There was a light burning in the kitchen and when he saw the dishes stacked everywhere he was momentarily bemused because, in recent weeks, while he turned night into day struggling to keep the family business afloat it had become an effort to even remember that he *had* a wife.

Now in the act of helping himself to some fresh orange juice from his extraordinarily well-stocked refrigerator, Sander remembered that Tally had asked him to come home to dinner. He dug out his mobile and recalled switching off the reminder he had programmed in at the club where he had entertained the Russians. He had meant to ring her when it was more convenient but had forgotten entirely. He swore and crossed the room to the dining table in the alcove, still laid with cutlery and glasses and a rather poignant little bud vase filled with a drooping posy. He stood gazing down at the trappings of the meal he had failed to show up for with a sinking heart and a conscience that was suddenly cutting him like a knife.

In the bedroom, Tally awoke when the fridge door slammed shut and she sat up, seeing the thin line of light below the door. Sander was home, Sander had actually bothered to *come* home! She scrambled off the bed, bemused to register that she was still wearing her high heels as she had fallen asleep on top of the duvet. Pushing her tumbling curls off her brow, she headed angrily into the lounge.

Sander focused on Tally in the doorway and he was staggered by her get-up: she never wore sexy lingerie for his benefit and tonight she had really pushed the boat out. Her beautiful breasts were foaming over the lace edge of a low-cut bra much racier than her usual selection, while a short robe of floral fabric barely covered skimpy high-cut knickers and did nothing at all to hide the length of leg on show. His body reacting involuntarily with all the powerful pent-up hunger of a male who had suppressed his sexual appetite for weeks, Sander dragged his attention from her wonderfully curvaceous body with the greatest difficulty.

'I owe you an apology, *moli mou*. I should've phoned,' he breathed, colliding with green eyes bright with angry condemnation…

CHAPTER TEN

THOSE words were too little too late to soothe Tally.

While she acknowledged that her threatened miscarriage had got their marriage off to a poor start, she had suffered her neglect in silence. She felt as if her body's show of weakness, which seemed to have made everything go wrong, was somehow *her* fault. She had made no demands and had voiced no complaints. Indeed she had attempted to be a supportive understanding partner, only to feel mortified by the obvious fact that her husband seemed neither to want her or need her in that role.

She did not feel like a wife and Sander didn't treat her like one either. He had made no attempt to spend time with her or to enquire into what she did with her days in a foreign city where she had no friends. Cosima had ignored both her sister's wedding and Tally's sending of her mobile phone number, making it clear that she did not want contact with her sibling even if she was currently living in the same country. Sander could not have made his lack of interest in Tally, his marriage and their future child more obvious and suddenly Tally could not credit that she had tolerated that indifference in silence for so long.

'You owe me more than an apology for the last month, you owe me an explanation—'

An ebony brow quirked. 'About what?'

Green eyes pure emerald with anger, Tally threw her hands out in a demonstration of the strong emotion rippling through her. 'You've treated me like the invisible woman ever since our wedding day. Why on earth did you marry me if you were planning to behave like that? What was the point?'

His deep-set dark eyes were heavy with exhaustion and his luxuriant lashes lowered to screen his wary gaze. He shifted a broad shoulder. 'I'm too tired for this stuff now. We'll discuss it tomorrow—'

'I probably won't see you tomorrow,' Tally interrupted. 'Or haven't you noticed that you walk out of here at dawn and don't come back much before dawn the next day?'

'I'm not in the mood for an argument—'

'I don't care!' Tally broke in with fiery persistence. 'I have the right to know where I stand. I have the right to ask you why the heck you married me when you don't seem to want me as a wife!'

Sander's big powerful body had pulled taut with tension and his stubborn mouth compressed as he shot her a sardonic glance. 'Let's not go into that.'

'Why not?'

'Because you might not like the answer I give you!' Sander slung back before he could think better of it, his temper rising in direct proportion to his exhaustion and his impatience and knocking him off guard. He was dead on his feet: all he wanted to do was sleep. Even the hard wooden floor was beginning to look inviting.

In receipt of that bewildering response, Tally had fallen very still. 'Why wouldn't I like it?'

'Leave it, Tally,' Sander urged in exasperation, striding past her to head into the bedroom she had just vacated.

'And what if I don't want to leave it?' Tally sped in his wake, refusing to back off.

'You'll wish you had,' Sander told her wryly, tossing his jacket and tie down on a chair. 'Look, I admit that you have grounds for complaint. So far, I've not been the most considerate husband, but tonight is not the time to call me to account for my mistakes. I'm too tired to talk right now. I've spent hours exchanging tall stories with a pair of Russian businessmen who could drink the Volga dry and still remain standing.'

'You can't throw something like that at me and then refuse to tell me the whole story.'

'There *is* no story,' Sander said flatly, standing still to unbutton his shirt.

'I want to know why you married me!'

'Well, not because you shout at three in the morning and demand answers that it would be a challenge for me to give you even if I was less tired,' Sander framed wearily.

'I deserve the truth,' Tally challenged. 'It seems

pretty obvious that you only married me because I'm pregnant.'

Sander grimaced. 'Tomorrow, Tally—'

'No, not tomorrow—*now*!' she fired back at him. 'Every step of this relationship you have controlled everything but now it's my turn. Why did you ask me to marry you?'

And in answer to that bold challenge, Sander was suddenly filled with such a swelling, unstoppable surge of rage that he could no longer hold the words back. 'Because your father threatened to bring down Volakis Shipping if I didn't!'

Assailed by an explanation so far from her expectations, Tally could only blink at him and stare in sheer bewilderment. 'Excuse me? My father? He threatened you? When did that happen? Did you tell him I was pregnant?'

'No. Someone—presumably you, your mother or even your half-sister—told Anatole about the baby, and that I was responsible. He was furious. He came to see me at my London office and demanded that I marry you. If I refused, he threatened to scare off a contract that Volakis Shipping needed to survive. Your father is an influential man in the world of business. He always has his ear to the ground. People who matter listen to his tips.'

The hectic flush in Tally's cheeks was slowly receding as shock drained the natural colour from her face. 'I wasn't the one who told him.' Slowly, numbly she shook her head in an emphatic negative to underline that point, but she was still so taken aback by what he had revealed that she could not yet put it all together inside her mind. 'And Cosima didn't even know I was pregnant which only leaves your parents or my mother, and if *she* told my father, I'm amazed, because as a rule she can hardly bear to speak to him.'

'My parents have said nothing. So it wasn't you who talked…you didn't run to tell stories so that your father would put pressure on me?' His shirt hanging open to reveal a muscular bronzed wedge of hair-roughened chest, Sander searched her revealing face with incisive dark eyes. He was impressed by her demeanour and convinced that she was telling him the truth. 'That does make me feel better.'

And Tally finally understood where the anger she had sensed in him from the outset of their marriage had come from and why it had lingered so that his bitterness soured everything between them. Naturally she could have done nothing to defuse that anger when he had chosen to keep such a massive secret from her. As comprehension sank in fully, though, she almost drowned in the flood tide of his cruelly unwelcome honesty and discovered that her shame was so great that she could no longer meet his dark golden gaze.

Her husband had been blackmailed into marrying her.

That was so horrendous, so truly unspeakable an act, that she felt as though she had been punched in the gut and was struggling without success to get air into her starved lungs. She was shaken that the father she barely knew could have so much influence that he could threaten Sander's family business, but she was equally shocked that her father could have cared enough about her future to even consider putting pressure on the father of her child to marry her. In fact, that did not make sense to her at all.

'My father doesn't love me,' Tally muttered with an unemotional acceptance of that truth that came from years of disappointed hopes. 'He did what the family court told him he had to do: he paid my living and educational expenses. But he very rarely wants to see me. I irritate him by reminding him of my mother and, as you saw, he didn't care enough to step out in public as my father and attend my wedding, although again he paid for it. So, bearing in mind that he doesn't really care about me at all, why would he force you to marry me?'

'In Anatole's eyes it was a matter of principle and honour. You being pregnant and unmarried was an affront to *his* dignity,' Sander explained grimly. 'Anatole Karydas is very conscious of his image.'

'He was saving face,' Tally traded flatly, recognising that her father's overweening sense of importance was the most likely explanation for his behaviour. 'Did he really have enough power to damage Volakis Shipping? I didn't realise he was that important.'

'A whisper in the wrong place would have killed

that contract. Unfortunately my late brother left the company in a much more vulnerable state than I had appreciated. I only learned how bad things were after our wedding. My father was in over his head; he's out of touch with the way business is done these days,' Sander admitted heavily. 'If I wasn't such a stubborn bastard, I would have offered my help long ago and we might have avoided the current crisis. Sadly, it took your father's threat to make me accept that blood is thicker than water.'

But Tally wasn't listening to that little speech or the ramifications of Sander's belated appreciation of the strength and importance of family ties. Shock had produced a spreading puddle of ice in the pit of her stomach and her skin felt cool and clammy. Glancing up, she caught a glimpse of her reflection in a mirror across the room and thought how horribly humiliating it was to be caught swanning round in sexy lingerie in an effort to attract a man who had clearly never really wanted her for more than the light entertainment factor of a few weeks. Add in a pregnancy that had proved equally undesirable and it was little wonder that he was avoiding intimacy. In haste, she walked into the dressing room to remove the wrap and shoes she was wearing. She took out trousers and a top and put them on, pushing her feet into flat comfortable shoes and burying the memory of the fancy underpinnings she still wore and why she had bought them.

It struck her as deeply ironic that she should ultimately have her uninterested parents to thank for her humiliation and heartbreak. Now, because her mind simply could not cope with the truth about her marriage, she looked back in time instead and recalled her mother's complacent rather than surprised response to the news that Sander had asked her daughter to marry him. Crystal had been triumphant and had undoubtedly told Anatole that Tally was pregnant. Her mother had probably enjoyed delivering that provocative news, possibly guessing how much it would annoy the older man that history was in danger of repeating itself in the next generation. Perhaps Anatole had feared that Tally's relationship to him would once again be publicly exposed to embarrass him, along with the news that Tally was also pregnant by a Greek tycoon. For whatever reasons, he had chosen to force Sander Volakis into marrying her by threatening the future of Volakis Shipping.

There was no bouncing back from such a devastating blow, Tally acknowledged bleakly. Sander had surrendered to blackmail to protect his family's business interests. But what else could he have done? She could only begin to imagine how tough Sander must've found it to allow anyone to force him into doing anything he didn't want to do. That must truly have been a case of mind over matter, for Sander was bone-deep proud, independent and stubborn.

Why on earth hadn't she suspected that something was badly wrong? When she contrasted Sander's reaction when she first told him she was pregnant to his behaviour a week later, when he had asked her to marry him, she marvelled that she had happily accepted his sudden change of heart. The sad truth was that he had told her what she most wanted to hear and she had trusted and believed in him on that basis. People rarely wanted to kill the messenger who brought what appeared to be good news.

'Tally…' The dressing-room door was slowly pushed back and Sander looked in at her, a frown line etched between his winged ebony brows, his lean, darkly handsome features taut as he towered over her smaller figure. 'Are you all right?'

Disturbingly aware that he had caught her in a moment of weakness, Tally straightened her slim shoulders and lifted her chin as she returned to the bedroom. 'Of course I am.'

But regardless of what she said, Sander could see that she was very far from being all right: her face was white and strained, her eyes were blank and evasive and she was trembling as if she was cold. Guilt assailed Sander in a rolling tide of discomfiture. He cursed his bluntness and regretted the sense of rancour that had pushed him into spilling the beans. Of course she was upset; what else had he expected?

Sander closed a hand over hers and used his strength to gently push her down on the side of the bed. 'You look as exhausted as I feel. It's too late to talk about this now. We'll sort everything out tomorrow,' he told her levelly. 'I'm going to have a shower and then I'm coming to bed.'

Tally nodded like a marionette but the instant the bathroom door closed she was on her feet again, hurrying into the dressing room to pull down a bag from an upper shelf. Tugging open drawers and racing around, she threw in clothing and keepsakes that she didn't want to leave behind. No doubt Sander could ensure that the remainder of her belongings were transported back to London for her. Her face was wet with tears and her heart was thumping far too fast with nerves by the time she had finished packing. She relaxed a little once she recognised that the shower was still running in the bathroom. Donning a jacket, she left the apartment and travelled down in the lift.

Their marriage, which had barely got off the ground, had crashed and burned and there was nothing left worth fighting for or talking about, Tally reflected wretchedly. He didn't love her; in the circumstances he couldn't even particularly *like* her! Evidently he had strongly suspected that she might have used her father to put pressure on him to offer her a wedding ring. If ever there was a last straw in a scenario, the sheer level of Sander's distrust in her had to be the final killing blow. He hadn't wanted to marry her. She could not trust one word that he had said the day he proposed, because self-evidently he had only said what he *had* to say to get her to the altar and protect Volakis Shipping from her father's threats.

The security man in the foyer got her a taxi that would take her to the airport. She sat in the back seat as the car travelled through dark lamplit streets and wondered how she was going to continue living in a world that no longer contained Sander. She wasn't supposed to love him like that when he didn't love her, but she had given up trying to explain the fiercely strong emotion she had felt for Sander from the moment she had met him. She might not have been happy living with him, but she knew she was going to be a great deal unhappier without him. At least while they'd still been together there had been hope that things might improve. Now? *Now* she was looking down a long, dark, empty tunnel and there was no light at all visible at the end of it.

She had forgotten that there was an airline strike. People were lying down and sitting everywhere and the queues were endless. After a long wait she learned that it would be eight hours before she could board a flight back to London. For the sake of a few hours she did not see the point of heading to a hotel. She was browsing through the shops to pass the time when she glanced up and saw Sander staring at her from across the concourse.

Aware that having told Tally the truth about their marriage had made him feel a lot less aggrieved, distrustful and tense, Sander had strolled back into their bedroom, weary but comparatively happy for a man at serious odds with his wife. And the first thing he had noticed was that the bed was empty and the lights were out in the hall. He had checked the lounge and then the second thing he'd noticed was the absence of the tiny jade frog Tally had placed on the dressing table. Her 'lucky' frog, which she took to exams and all important occasions—it was gone. He had looked into the dressing room and breathed in deep when he'd seen clear evidence of hasty packing.

Shock had roared through Sander then in a blinding wave. Tally had walked out on him; he couldn't believe it, didn't *want* to believe it! Tally had one priceless trait he had always taken very much for granted, but which he greatly admired. He saw her as unique amongst the women of his experience—she was a really good sport, who could usually be depended on to do the sensible thing. She was not impulsive or foolish, nor was she given to going off on emotional tangents.

Until you told her that her father had made you marry her.

That was the instant when it dawned on Sander that he had expected a little too much. Simultaneously, he was also remembering his life in London with Tally. A life laced with the warmth, fun, enthusiasm and spirit that were so much a part of her vitality and her genuine interest in what he did every day. His thoughts cut back across the absence of newer memories created since their wedding and went straight to an image of life *without* Tally. For the very first time since he had met her, Sander realised that he had moved on from the constant late nights, the wild parties and the procession of ever-changing women he had once bedded. He had moved on without ever realising the fact. He had even begun to occasionally think about the baby…

It was the work of a moment for Sander to plunge back to his feet and take action, shedding the towel and dragging out clothes with more haste than cool. Before he left the apartment he went into the depths of a drawer to remove an item he had bought earlier that week. It was small, insignificant and cheap, an impulse buy that had embarrassed him in retrospect but it was also, he hoped, a symbol for a more committed future. The security guard on the ground floor gave Sander's unshaven, dishevelled appearance a knowing masculine appraisal that set Sander's even white teeth on edge and while hailing another taxi for his employer confirmed—without being asked—Tally's destination. Sander briefly toyed with the idea of saying he wasn't heading to the airport as well and then thought about his empty apartment again and all false pride somehow fell away.

It wasn't that he minded living alone; he was *used* to living alone. Furthermore he liked his freedom, his own space. It was just that he had become accustomed to Tally being there in his space, he reasoned feverishly, conscious of a looming edge of panic foreign to his experience. The candles round the bath, the cushions on his sleek leather sofas, the endearing, perfectly spelled and long-winded texts that made him smile no matter how busy he was.

Tally was his wife. Strange how he had never allowed himself to think about her in that guise until now when it might well be too late, he conceded heavily. Had he treated her like the invisible woman? That was a fair point, he had to admit. Without warning though he was plunged into a welter of surprisingly familiar recollections. He had noticed her presence in his life much more than he had been prepared to admit. The scent of her perfume and the orange soap she loved, her passion for peanuts and her music playing in the bedroom while he watched the business news and withstood the temptation to join her. It crossed his mind that had he fought the temptation a little less hard his wife might not have run away.

Women never ran out on Sander and he had long since worked out why Oleia had let him down so badly when he was a teenager. He had adored Oleia Telis but falling in love with her had made him boring, soppy and needy. There again, love had never done Sander any favours, which was why he had always fought hard to stay untouched and detached from an emotion likely to drag him down and sap his strength and peace of mind. His earliest memories of childhood were rooted in disturbing images of his mother pushing him away irritably and calling him 'clingy' and 'babyish'. The rejections had been continual, yet somehow his brother had never come in for the same treatment. Sander had soon learned independence, while also learning to equate love with pain and weakness and the risk of exploitation.

'Tally...'

Paralysed to the spot beside a magazine stand,

Tally stared at Sander's tall powerful figure as he strode towards her. She was shocked by the sight of him because it had not occurred to her that he might follow her. And, for once, his reputation for sartorial elegance was under threat. He was wearing well-worn jeans teamed with an open shirt and a black designer suit jacket. His strong jaw line was dark with stubble, highlighting the wilful beauty of his wide sensual mouth, and his black hair had dried all spiky and tousled. 'What are you doing here?'

Sander pushed impatient fingers through his untidy black hair and breathed almost argumentatively, '*You're* here!' as if that answered everything.

'That doesn't explain why you followed me,' Tally persisted, colliding with stunning golden-brown eyes and hurriedly looking away, even while her breath hitched in her throat and her heart began to race.

'Look, we can't talk here,' Sander intoned, closing an arm round her taut spine to ease her out of the path of a man pushing past. 'We'll get coffee—'

'Haven't you noticed that this place is in turmoil with the strike? Everywhere is packed. There are no seats,' Tally protested, sliding away from physical contact with him like an electrified eel. 'I don't think we have anything to talk about, Sander. After what you told me, our marriage is null and void.'

'How can it be null and void? You're carrying my child!' Sander shot back at her quick as a flash.

Tally was so disconcerted by that response from a male who never ever mentioned her condition if he could help it that she stared at him. A dark rise of blood accentuated his superb cheekbones as he recognised her incredulity. He veiled his stunning dark eyes and closed a hand that brooked no argument over one of hers to draw her over to the edge of a crowded café. There he set her free and she looked on in amazement as he approached a couple of young men at a table and, withdrawing his wallet, made it worth their while to give up the table. He then retrieved her and sat her down with great determination. 'Give me five minutes.'

You're carrying my child!

Had that only finally sunk in? Tally was very much shaken by his appearance at the airport. It had taken all her courage and the conviction that she was doing the right thing to walk out on Sander and their marriage. She had assumed he would be relieved that she had chosen to leave without any histrionics. That he might choose instead to look that gift horse in the mouth and chase after her was a complete surprise.

Sander reappeared and set a cup of tea in front of her, a beaker of strong black coffee gripped in his other hand. The strain in his gorgeous dark golden eyes was palpable, the line of his eloquent mouth compressed with the level of his fierce tension.

'I just don't understand what you're doing here,' Tally whispered truthfully. 'It would be easier for you just to let me go.'

'I can't let you go,' Sander ground out abruptly.

'Sander! For the past month you have behaved as if I didn't exist while I was living below the same roof,' Tally reminded him bluntly.

'It wasn't deliberate. I'm not like you in relationships…I don't think things through. I didn't have a plan as I do in business,' Sander advanced in a sudden flood of driven words, his beautiful eyes full of an appeal for her to listen. 'I was just so *angry*—'

'I know. I understand that,' Tally broke in, because she did.

'I was just living with the rage and Volakis Shipping was failing,' he told her in a raw undertone, black lashes screening his gaze as he gulped down black coffee.

'Even though I assume that that contract which my father originally threatened went through?'

'The TKR contract did, but I'm afraid that that was just the tip of the iceberg. I was scared I had left it too late. I wasn't sure I *could* save the company,' Sander admitted doggedly, behaving as though every word of that confession were being dragged from him under torture, for owning up to doubts and insecurities was something he never did. 'So, I wasn't really thinking about our marriage the last few weeks.'

And Tally got the point, she really did. Business had come first when it forced him to marry her, and business had come first when in spite of that huge sacrifice of his freedom he had discovered that the family company might still go down. That unhappy truth must only have added to his outrage at the position he was in. She understood that perfectly.

On the other side of the table, Sander was talking into his mobile phone at a fast rate of knots. Without warning, he leapt up. 'Come on,' he urged, reaching down and taking charge of her cabin case.

'Come on…where?' she exclaimed.

'I've found us a hotel. This…' Sander sent speaking dark impatient eyes over their crowded surroundings and barely repressed a shudder. '*This* is impossible!'

Tally was willing to admit that an airport café was not the best place to stage so private a dialogue, but she was reluctant to go to a hotel with him. 'I just don't think we have anything left to talk about,' she protested, almost running to keep up with his long stride.

Already fed up with talking, Sander stopped dead and reached for her instead. He hauled her up against him and bent his handsome dark head to crush her soft full lips beneath his. She tasted like strawberries and wine, hot and heady and sweeter than sweet, and his senses reeled in a seething surge of excitement. An agony and an ecstasy of feeling and sensation roared through Tally's slim body with such intensity that she trembled. It had been so long since he touched her that she could not restrain a gasp when his tongue pierced the tender sensitivity of her mouth and the thought of a much more intimate possession turned her secret places to melted honey and left her knees shaking.

His hand curved to her hip and rocked her up against him so that she could feel the hard thrust of his erection. Golden eyes ablaze with sexual heat gazed down into her hectically flushed face expectantly.

'Yes…yes, we *do* need to talk!' Tally exclaimed abruptly, sensing that not talking and using the hotel room for a far more basic purpose would come far more naturally to him at that moment. 'But that's *all*.'

She knew it was crazy to let Sander walk her

out of the airport and into a taxi to travel to a nearby hotel, but she was on automatic pilot and desperately, cravenly hoping and praying that he might have something to say that she might want to hear. She had her ticket for her flight and there was nothing to stop her from still boarding that plane, she reminded herself urgently. At the hotel she discovered that he had booked them into a penthouse suite because that was the only accommodation available.

'I understand that you've spent the last month fighting to keep Volakis Shipping in business,' she conceded, standing by a floor-deep window to look across the spacious reception room at him. 'But you didn't tell me about it until I'd already walked out. How can we have a future together when you won't even share something that basic with me?'

Sander pondered that question and his ebony brows drew together in a frown line. 'It's easy to share when things are going well, but when it's the other way round, talking about it makes me feel...' he shrugged awkwardly '...wimpy,' he finally pronounced with complete contempt.

'So I'm only allowed to hear good news on the business front? Sander…' Momentarily her voice trailed away and she semi-groaned to express her discomfiture, turning reproachful eyes on him to say, 'You actually thought I might have put my father up to blackmailing you into marrying me.'

Sander strode forward. 'The instant I saw your face when I said that I knew it wasn't true!'

Tally was relieved by his immediate withdrawal of that suspicion. 'But how could you even think I was capable of that kind of manipulation?'

'Blame the world I live in, *moli mou*. People use whatever weapon they can find to get on in life.'

'But that's not who I am, that's not what I'm about,' Tally argued with pained sincerity.

'I used to believe that and then, when you fell pregnant, I had doubts. Your father's blackmail made me doubt you even more, but I couldn't risk a confrontation with you before the wedding to satisfy myself on that score.'

With reluctance, Tally accepted that he could not have come clean with her at that stage. But she had so many other concerns that the silence simmered.

'Throw whatever you have to throw,' Sander urged in raw encouragement. 'Bring it—I can take it.'

'Feeling as you have to feel about being rail-roaded into our marriage, why on earth have you come after me?' Tally demanded emotively. 'Why didn't you just let me go?'

'Because I *can't*!' Sander proclaimed without hesitation. 'I thought of my life before I met you and I don't miss any aspect of it. I don't want my freedom back, I want you to stay with me.'

'You feel bad about the way this has happened. I think that's your conscience talking.'

'If I thought I would be happier if you left Greece, I wouldn't be here asking you to stay,' Sander told her with an assurance that was per-suasive. 'I'm not that much of a fool.'

Exhaustion catching up with her, Tally sank heavily down on a seat. 'You don't love me. Look at it from my point of view: what would I stay for?'

Sander studied her small determined figure

with brooding force. He wondered how he could explain why he wanted her when he couldn't explain it even to his own satisfaction. As he watched her chin came up, corkscrew curls the colour of marmalade dancing back from her cheekbones and enhancing evocative green eyes.

With a stifled curse he lifted his lean brown hands to inscribe an arc of frustration in the air and he broke the simmering silence. 'I don't do love but there's a whole host of other things I can offer you, *pedhi mou*,' he argued vehemently, a muscle snapping taut at the corner of his stubborn sensual mouth. 'I'll be there for you when you're lonely or scared or ill. There won't be any other woman in my life. I won't let business come between us again. I'll make time for us to be together. You will be the centre of my world and I will spoil you and the baby, that I promise you.'

Sander spoke with far more emotion than she had ever heard him use before and the rough edge to his dark deep drawl and the strain in his beautiful dark eyes added another whole layer of sincerity to that speech. Tally was impressed and her heart was touched. She was even more pleased to hear his reference to the child she carried. He was offering to care for her as she had once believed he cared for her and it crossed her mind that had it not been for the distressing effect of her father's blackmail Sander might never have stopped caring for her.

'You never mention the baby,' she remarked awkwardly.

Sander dug his hand into a pocket and removed something, which he extended to her. 'I bought it a couple of weeks ago. I saw it in a window.'

Tally accepted the little brightly painted metal train and her eyes burned and prickled with a surge of moisture. It was an elaborate adult toy built of tiny components and would have been ridiculously dangerous to give to a young child. But Sander had no notion of such safety hazards and with this particular purchase it was very much the thought that had prompted it that counted.

'I mean, girls can play with trains too,' Sander added in forceful addition, keen to let her know that he wasn't being sexist.

'Of course they can,' she agreed gruffly, her throat aching.

You will be the centre of my world. That, and a promise of fidelity would be enough for her, Tally reflected fiercely. Love would have been the icing on the cake, love would have made everything perfect, but she knew that she didn't live in a perfect world and she had not yet given up all hope. Maybe some day he would fall in love with her.

Sander closed his arms round her and almost squeezed the oxygen from her lungs as he crushed her to him in a driven embrace that said far more about his troubled and vulnerable state of mind than his words. 'I want you to be my wife. I want you to be a permanent part of my life, *pedhi mou*,' he swore feelingly. 'And I promise that you won't regret staying with me.'

'I'd better not,' Tally told him tightly, fighting the emotion threatening to paralyse her vocal cords, when she saw the suspicious glimmer of moisture in his beautiful dark eyes and realised that he too was fighting to control strong feelings. 'But you'll have to be on your very best behaviour.'

Sander loosened his grip, only long enough to stoop and sweep her right off her feet into his arms and grin down at her. 'Absolutely.'

'I expect action in the bedroom *every* night,' Tally warned him, reddening but desperate to take the tension out of the atmosphere.

She was rewarded by his dazzling grin. 'If only you knew how hard it was to keep my distance, but every time I was tempted I thought about the blackmail and I felt like I was being controlled by your father. That just made me angry again,' he admitted gruffly.

'But you're not angry any more,' Tally pointed out soothingly, reaching up a caressing hand to his strong jaw line as he laid her down on a wide divan bed in the bedroom.

Sander shed his jacket and came down beside her and she hugged him tight, her heart racing. He felt the terrible tension seep out of him and he held her close, one hand smoothing back her hair from her face.

'I have a house in the South of France. It belonged to Titos and he left it to me in his will. We never had a honeymoon and I think it's time I remedied that, *pedhi mou*,' Sander murmured. 'At the very least, we'll stay there for a few weeks and make a fresh start—'

'A fresh start begins in *here*,' Tally argued, pressing his broad chest over his heart in emphasis. 'It doesn't matter where we are, just that we're together—together in body and spirit.'

Sander cupped her chin and gazed deep in her shining eyes, marvelling at the strength of her optimistic spirit while experiencing a blessed sense of peace that was new to his restless nature. 'I *do* care about you: the last month is just a blur of meetings and late nights. I've been very selfish. I *am* very selfish, *matia mou*,' he concluded in apologetic warning, anxious dark eyes skimming to her from below spiky dark lashes.

'I knew you weren't perfect. But I signed up for the long haul,' Tally whispered unevenly, loving him so much as she met his dark steady gaze that tears were only seconds away in the great tide of emotion sweeping through her.

Sander looked down at her. 'Just don't give up on me. I can learn, I can do everything better.'

Tally rested a fingertip against his sculpted lips. 'It's not a competition.'

'Competition brings out the best in me.' He sighed.

Love surged inside her but she crammed it back, refusing to say those words. Declarations of love always came with expectations attached and she didn't want to do that to him. He had said openly, honestly, that he didn't do love but that he did do caring and she promised herself that that was going to be enough to make her happy long term. He pressed a kiss to her lips and she tingled, inside and out, her body awakening after a long period of frustration.

'We're both so tired,' Tally whispered ruefully.

'But I won't sleep until I feel that you're mine again,' Sander asserted, quietly removing her clothes with careful hands, while shedding his own with a good deal less concern.

And he was very gentle, slow and skilled and she reached a climax of breathtaking splendour and knew a happiness that made her cry. He held her close and teased her for her runaway emotions while secretly appreciating the sheer womanly tenderness of her heart. She was everything he had never thought he would want and now that he had her back he was fiercely determined never to lose her again. In that moment he had so many good intentions he was bursting with them.

'Go to sleep,' he urged her tenderly when she yawned and snuggled closer.

And Tally drifted off to sleep in the cradle of his strong arms, every fear of the future overcome at last.

Four months later, Tally finished hanging new curtains in the oak-floored salon of the house in the South of France, which they had made their main home, and straightened her aching back with a sigh of relief.

Sander's brother's house had needed a great deal of work before it could be considered either comfortable or presentable. Having bought the rundown property as an investment, Titos had never got around to fixing it up. Tally had fallen madly in love with the old farmhouse, which was crying out for a designer's hand, and room by room she had worked through the house, setting a loving stamp on every corner of it.

'Sander said you weren't to climb any more ladders,' Binkie reminded the younger woman disapprovingly from the doorway.

Tally tried not to grin. Sander's all-male habit of laying down the law and the pronouncements and prohibitions he uttered perfectly matched Binkie's old-fashioned expectations of a husband. Binkie had consented to come and work for them as a housekeeper after Crystal had decided that she no longer needed the older woman's services in London. Tally had seen less of her mother since Crystal moved in with her current boyfriend, Roger, a widowed furniture manufacturer, who lived in Monaco. Crystal, however, seemed happy and more content with Roger than she had been for quite some time. In the same period Tally had heard nothing at all from her father, Anatole, and she wasn't expecting that situation to change.

'I was only climbing a little set of steps, not a proper ladder,' Tally reasoned quietly.

'You're pregnant, you have to take care.' The older woman sighed. 'You should have asked me or called Marcel to help.'

Tally smiled noncommittally as she recalled Marcel the gardener's aghast response to being asked to do anything indoors and Binkie had always been very nervous of using steps or ladders. She might now be six months pregnant, Tally acknowledged, but she was perfectly healthy and felt strong and well. She smoothed a protective hand over the swell of her tummy and smiled warmly as a little fluttering sensation indicated that her child was moving inside her. When the baby went quiet and she didn't feel his movements, she always worried. Her baby might not be born yet but Tally was already convinced that she loved him. At the last scan she had learned that her baby was a boy and she was delighted. She didn't care whether she had a boy or a girl and simply prayed for a healthy child.

Most days she took a dreamy tour of the room she had already lovingly decorated and furnished as a nursery in bright shades of lemon and blue. She could hardly wait to welcome their son into the world and could now scarcely recall a time when she had worried about Sander's commitment to being a parent.

Sander had kept all his promises, Tally acknowledged with a sunny smile, her heart lifting at the thought that the husband she adored would be returning from a three-day business trip to Athens that very evening. Since that day when Sander had reclaimed her from the airport, their marriage had gone from strength to strength and he had made her the centre of his world. He shared his workday frustrations with her and there had been many, for he and his father were uneasy work colleagues and Volakis Shipping was still fighting to attain long-term security.

For the greater part of the week, Sander was based in France and he ran the family company and his own business interests from a distance. The board of directors had recognised his genius in the changes he had made in how the business operated and had infuriated his competitive father by giving Sander a rousing vote of confidence in reward. Sander and Tally both enjoyed the more relaxed pace of life in France and often had his friends to stay at the weekend. Tally enjoyed being a hostess and was now a good deal less intimidated by the beautiful girls who threw themselves at Sander's head every chance they got.

After all, Tally knew her husband much better than she had known him when they first married. She had learned that he was not a fan of women who chased him and disliked such bold approaches. He also had no love for clubs and noisy parties and much preferred social occasions attended only by close friends.

He would be wild to take her to bed when he got home that night, Tally savoured with hot cheeks and a sliding sensation of anticipation between her thighs. Her husband was highly sexed and she was still shaken by the hot rush of excitement that just a look or a touch from Sander could awaken in her.

Two hours later, Sander strode into the house and flung down his raincoat. Coming home to Tally was always an occasion and his gaze centred on her small, curvy figure standing beside the tall glittering Christmas tree. The house was a festive wonderland of Christmas ornamentation and, as the son of parents who had only ever celebrated the season in the most low-key and tasteful manner, Sander was impressed by his wife's wonderful homemaking skills.

Her green eyes were bright with welcome and tenderness and he headed straight for her and scooped her up against him to kiss her with passionate appreciation. Her heart racing, Tally kissed Sander back with unconcealed enthusiasm.

'How much time have we got before dinner?' he breathed raggedly against her reddened lips.

Angling the swell of her stomach away from him, Tally shimmied her hip in wanton invitation against his lean powerful frame. 'Enough time,' she assured him shamelessly, for she had planned it that way, aware that Sander would only really relax after they had made love again.

Meeting green eyes dancing with merriment and mischief, Sander laughed with unashamed masculine appreciation. He was truly happy to be home again as he walked her down to the bedroom they shared. Clothes were shed without ceremony and the kisses grew hotter than hot very quickly. Their impatience to reacquaint their bodies and sate the craving for satisfaction that tormented them both when they were parted for a few days lent an added edge of excitement. In the aftermath, her heart slowly returning to a less accelerated beat, Tally feasted her eyes on her husband's lean, dark devastating features and whispered, 'I missed you.'

Sander dropped another kiss on her soft full mouth and luxuriated in her embrace. 'Once the baby's born you'll be able to come with me, *pedhi mou.*'

Tally winced at that forecast. 'Babies like routine. I doubt if our baby will travel well.'

'My son will,' Sander forecast with perceptible pride. 'To be a Volakis is to be a good traveller by air or by sea.'

Tally giggled. 'Is that so?'

'Of course it is. My son will be clever and he will naturally want to please his father.'

Tally half sat up and gazed lovingly down at the father of her child before saying with her usual common sense, 'You're always disagreeing with yours.'

'But I will be a more caring parent and my son and I will have a closer relationship. I was always extra to requirements in my own family,' Sander told her with a dismissive shrug that did not quite conceal his regret that it should have been that way.

'You know...' Tally trailed gentle appreciative fingers across one stunning masculine cheek-bone '...you *are* my world.'

Sander caught her hand in his and kissed her fingertips. 'And you are at the very heart of mine, *kardoula mou*. I will always be grateful to your father for ensuring that I married you... what a treasure I might have missed out of my own ignorance and immaturity!'

And Tally recognised then that all his anger on that score was really laid to rest and their relationship had turned full circle. The warmth of his acceptance and his recognition of their increasingly close ties filled her to overflowing with happiness and contentment. In spite of all her careful planning dinner was very, very late that night...

* * * * *

The Volakis Vow
A marriage made of secrets...
An enthralling two-part story by bestselling author, Lynne Graham

This month:
THE MARRIAGE BETRAYAL

Tally Spencer, an ordinary girl with no experience of relationships...Sander Volakis, an impossibly rich and handsome Greek entrepreneur. Their worlds collide in an explosion of attraction and passion. Sander's expecting to love her and leave her, but for Tally this is love at first sight. Both are about to find that it's not easy to walk away...because Tally is expecting Sander's baby and he is being blackmailed into making her his wife!

Next month, look out for:
BRIDE FOR REAL

Just when they thought their hasty marriage was finished, Tally and Sander are drawn back together and the passion between them is just as strong… But Sander has hidden reasons for wanting his wife in his bed again, and Tally also has a terrible secret…and neither are prepared for what this tempestuous reunion will bring…

Available in November and December— can you wait to find out what happens? Here's a delicious taste of what you can expect...

PROLOGUE

BRILLIANT dark eyes grim, Sander studied the photo of his wife, looking small and sinuously sexy in a scarlet evening gown—and wrapped in another man's arms.

He was disturbed to appreciate that he was in shock. The white heat of the rage that followed made him light-headed and scoured him inside like a cleansing flame, leaving him feeling curiously hollow. Robert Miller, well, that wasn't a surprise, was it? Sander had noted at the Westgrave Manor party two years earlier that Miller had wanted Tally the minute he'd laid eyes on her. Just as Sander had, once. But in spite of his simmering fury, Sander pushed the newspaper away with a careless hand. He glanced at his watching father to say lightly like a practised card player hiding his hand, *'So?'*

'When will you be fully free of her?' Petros Volakis demanded sourly, as if an estranged wife, whose new single life was being fully documented by the media, was an embarrassment to the family name.

'I'm free now,' Sander pointed out with a shrug, for, although divorce proceedings still had a way to go, an official separation was already in place.

As his attention roamed involuntarily back to the newspaper lying close by, he questioned the strength of his reaction to seeing Tally with someone else. They were getting a divorce. It should be no surprise that she was back on the social circuit. But, like a man forced to stand still while hot pitch was slowly dripped onto his skin, Sander was in torment. Why? Prior to their break-up Tally had brandished her indifference to Sander like a banner and he had assumed that no man could breach her barriers. The idea that another man might have succeeded where he had failed outraged and challenged him.

'I don't see you featuring in the gossip columns the way you did before you married,' the older man remarked with more insight than Sander usually ascribed to him.

'I've grown up,' Sander countered drily. 'I'm also more discreet.'

'*She* was a mistake but we'll say no more about it,' Petros commented, noting the hardening of his son's stubborn jaw line with a wary eye.

His lean, darkly handsome face uninformative, Sander *had* nothing to say, at least nothing worth saying. He marvelled that his parents, who had not even offered him sympathy on the death of his firstborn son, could think that any aspect of his marriage could be their business. But then, relations had long been chilly between Sander and his parents. His elder brother, Titos, the family favourite, had died in a tragic accident and, although it was only thanks to Sander that Volakis Shipping had since recovered from his brother's disastrous management, Sander was still being made to feel a very poor second best in the son stakes. And now, all of a sudden, he was disturbingly conscious that his meteoric triumphs in business were in stark contrast to a frankly abysmal rating in his private life.

Tally, however, had moved on from their marriage at startling speed and was evidently enjoying considerable success: new business, new home, *new man*. That knowledge infuriated Sander, who remembered a much more innocent Tally, a glowing girl who had once been too excited to breathe when he kissed her. He could not stand to think of her in bed with Robert Miller and the awareness shocked him because he had never seen himself as a possessive man…

* * * * *

Don't forget to come back
at the beginning of next month
to find out what happens to Tally and Sander!

Mills & Boon® Large Print

November 2011

THE MARRIAGE BETRAYAL
Lynne Graham

THE ICE PRINCE
Sandra Marton

DOUKAKIS'S APPRENTICE
Sarah Morgan

SURRENDER TO THE PAST
Carole Mortimer

HER OUTBACK COMMANDER
Margaret Way

A KISS TO SEAL THE DEAL
Nikki Logan

BABY ON THE RANCH
Susan Meier

GIRL IN A VINTAGE DRESS
Nicola Marsh

Mills & Boon® Large Print
December 2011

BRIDE FOR REAL
Lynne Graham

FROM DIRT TO DIAMONDS
Julia James

THE THORN IN HIS SIDE
Kim Lawrence

FIANCÉE FOR ONE NIGHT
Trish Morey

AUSTRALIA'S MAVERICK MILLIONAIRE
Margaret Way

RESCUED BY THE BROODING TYCOON
Lucy Gordon

SWEPT OFF HER STILETTOS
Fiona Harper

MR RIGHT THERE ALL ALONG
Jackie Braun